STEAMY NIGHTS

A STEAMY, SMALL-TOWN ROMANTIC SUSPENSE

SERVICEMEN OF BLOSSOM SPRINGS

PJ FIALA

To the lovely women of my reader group, PJ Fiala's Road Queens, who help me out with names of characters, places, and businesses, thank you. I appreciate you and adore you.

Characters
Tjuana Brown - Micaela
Amy Burkhart - William's Hardware Store (series)
Vickie Chaisson - Travis Murphy (Grace's brother)
Karen Cranford LeBeau - Sid Hoffman (Book 1 Hero)
Alison Dinsmore - Roark Dinsmore (City Council President of Blossom Springs)
Kim Kurtz - Quinn Kurtz (Book 3 Hero)
Gayle Lazur - Jared Kurtz (Quinn Kurtz's son)
Arlene Miklovic - Theresa (server at the Sandbar)
Elinda Moody - Erin Moody (Police Officer)
Julia Murphy - Grace Murphy (Book 1 Heroine)
Terra Oenning - Hanna Valentine (Book 3 Heroine)
Terra Oenning - Hayes Brooks - (works for Quinn)
Ginny Pearson - Bodie (Gas Station Owner)
Julie Price - Margot Price (Book 2 Heroine)
Alisa Voss Forpahl - Isak Voss (Police Officer)
Jo West - Jace Marriott (Book 2 Hero); Tray Fielding (Police officer)

Carolyn Wolf McCutcheon - Cooper Wolf - Old guy who owns the garage (Book 1)
Dana Zamora - Hayden Lucht (Works for Quinn Kurtz)

Springs

Springs
HAND DRAWN BY PJ FIALA
The Sandbar Ranch
Tanning Parlor
Police Station
VFW
Supper Club
Hotel
Bank
Barber Shop
Williams Hardware
Groceries
Ice Cream
Insurance
Laundro-mat
Bait
Vet Clinic
Shannon Canning
Bluff Road
Sid & Sons
Bluff House Tavern Parking
City Hall
Court House
Bank
Maple Square
Flowers
Hair
Gas
Miracle Garage
Craft Mall
Alley
Classified
Jace Harrell
Bookkeepers
Tax
Thrift Shop
Sarge's Sandbar
Furniture of
The Beach
Boat Slips
Space
Tiki Bar
Condo
Condo
Condo
Sid Hoffman
Condo
Tony Bruno
Sunset Beach Road
Grace's Place
Grace's Place
Public Access to Beach
Jake Black
Barn

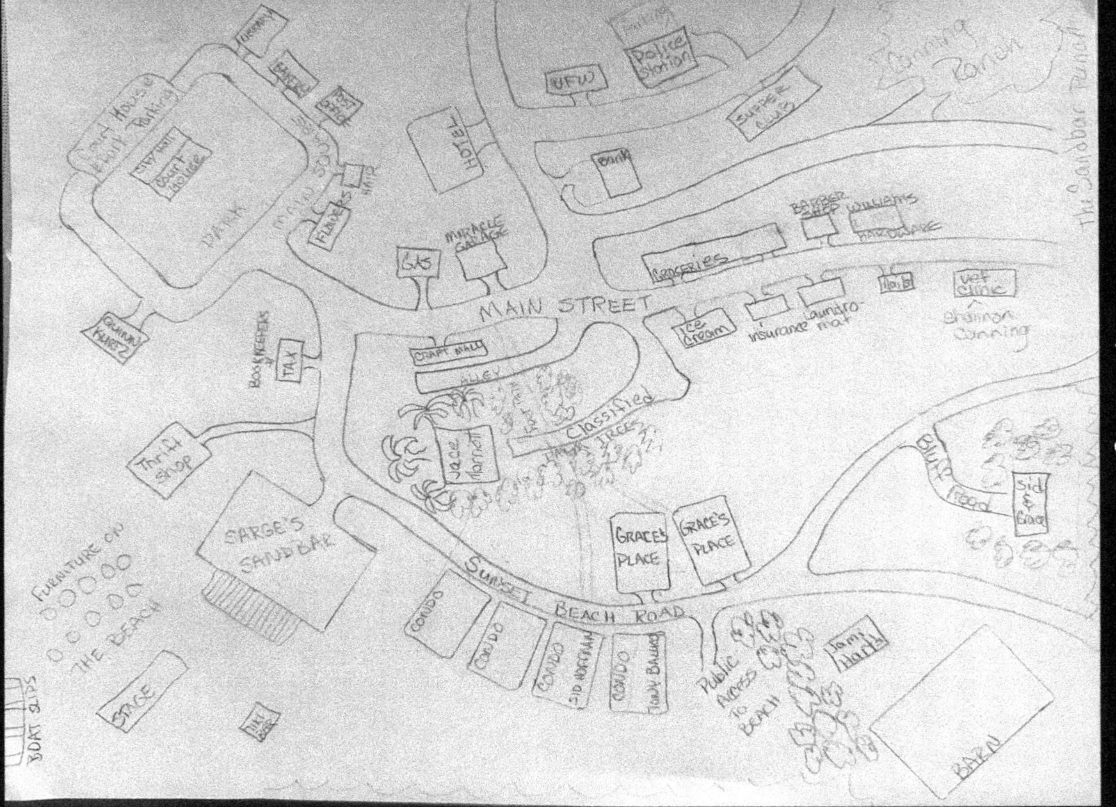

DESCRIPTION

He's convinced he's discovered an ideal paradise.

She's certain she's found her new beginning...

Together, they must fight to keep their new dreams alive.

Sid Hoffman, has suffered from PTSD since his time in Afghanistan. Inner peace has escaped him for years. Attending a bachelor party in Blossom Springs is a true awakening for him. Buying a garage and spending his days working with his hands has brought him more tranquility than he ever imagined.

Grace Murphy left an abusive relationship to follow her dream of owning short-term rentals. She's self-sufficient and ready to prove she has what it takes to build a thriving business and healthy life.

When outsiders roll into town and threaten their sanctuary, Sid and Grace join forces and fight to keep Blossom Springs the sanctuary they know it can be. Falling in love is the last thing these opposites were prepared for.

***

USA Today bestselling author PJ Fiala brings you the Servicemen of Blossom Springs series—heroes willing to sacrifice everything in service to their country, and for the men and women they love. A novel with no cliffhanger, no cheating, and a happily-ever-after guaranteed.

Let's stay in contact, join my newsletter so I can let you know about new releases, sales, promotions and more. https://www.subscribepage.com/pjfialafm

Sid finished dressing in his usual: a t-shirt, today's was blue, and his tan cargo shorts. He liked the pockets. A person needed pockets. He tucked his phone into his back right pocket. The keys to his little rented bungalow on the beach, thanks to his friend Jace, into the front left pocket. His wallet found a home in the leg pocket on the right side. And he had some loose change that landed in the left leg pocket. He liked hearing it jingle as he walked.

A quick look at his profile in the full-length mirror on the closet door, showed his belly had grown soft and his hair was streaked with gray. He was good with that though. At fifty-one, he still looked better than many. And, he'd worked hard to stay minimally in shape. Actually, he didn't work that hard, he just struggled to be hungry.

He shrugged and stepped outside. The small porch attached to his bungalow kept most of the sand out of the inside. His eyes focused first on the water. The morning sun always looked soft on the water. It was the setting sun that dazzled. No boats were visible yet today. No bikini-clad women hanging out on the sandbar. They'd come in droves this weekend though. That was his favorite part of visiting here. That, the low rent on the little bungalow, and his friends, Jace and Quinn close by.

He walked across the sand to the road out front, then set his pace to walk the length of Main Street, around to a back street or two, then make his way back. He always tried to put in two miles in the morning. But, soon he'd need to figure out how long he'd be staying here and where he'd go next.

Turning the corner, he stepped onto the sidewalk on Main Street. He set his pace for his normal stride, eager to see the sleepy town early in the morning. He hadn't ventured this way since he'd gotten here this week. The roar of motorcycles disturbed the quiet morning as they neared. The far end of town rumbled with their motors. He huffed out a deep breath. He loved a Harley or two, but goodness, this morning he was looking forward to the peace and quiet of this little town and the jingle of the change in his pocket.

He stepped off the curb at the first intersection, which was only controlled by four stop signs. The bright red octagon signs seemed out of place in this little town. They should have been muted colors and made of wood. It would fit the aesthetic better.

Moving to the next section of sidewalk, he stopped when he saw an old 1935 Harley Davidson Knucklehead sitting outside of an old garage. The large white peeling sign above the garage door said, *Garage* in large cursive letters which used to be blue. Sid chuckled. He turned his eyes back to the Harley. It had seen better days. The seat was cracked and peeling, the seat pan showed through, and rust had covered the exposed area.

He squatted to take a good look at the old Knuckle-head motor. It was always his favorite. He'd always wanted an old bike like this to scoot around on. But, his ex-wife refused to hear of it and he'd caved to her pressure. Then she left with nearly everything they owned, he kept all the money he'd earned, and he'd only rented places since. No place to work on an old bike like this.

An older voice broke into his musings. "That old bike has been sitting in that spot right there for about twenty some-odd years now."

Sid turned to see an old man, gray hair that sprung from his head at odd angles. His old, wrinkled thumbs hooked onto the straps of his bib overalls. His wrinkled hands wore grease and smudge from working on the vehicle on the hoist inside.

"Why is it sitting here?" Sid asked.

"Ah, well, the owner dropped it off, right where it sits right now and asked for it to be fixed. The motor seized up and he didn't know what to do about it. He and his buddy loaded it up on a trailer and brought it here. I told him it would cost a fair amount, and usually a seized motor stays just that way. He didn't have the money and didn't want the bike back. I always thought I'd fix it, but never had the danged time."

Sid walked around the old bike once more and nodded. "I get not having the time. It would take a bit of work, but I can get that bike running."

The old man laughed. "It would be a miracle if you could get that old thing running again."

Sid chuckled. He held out his right hand toward the old guy, "My name is Sid Hoffman."

An old, wrinkled hand grabbed onto his hand and shook. "Name's Cooper Wolf."

"Nice to meet you, Cooper."

"It's nice meeting you, Sid. So you like old bikes?"

"I like this old bike."

Cooper stared at the bike for a long while, Sid did too. "As I said, it'd be a miracle."

"I'll show you a miracle."

Cooper burst out laughing. His hands held his rounded belly as he did. "Okay, Sid Hoffman, miracle worker. You show me what you've got. If you can get it started, you can keep it."

Sid held his hand out again, "Shake on it?"

Cooper chuckled once more and shook Sid's hand. "Good luck, miracle worker. You're free to use my tools and my garage. Whatever you need, help yourself."

"Thank you, Mr. Wolf."

"Cooper or Coop."

Sid nodded as Coop limped back into the garage. The man must have been in his upper seventies. Still worked for a living. Typical of his generation, they didn't know how to not work. But, they were a dying breed for sure.

He inhaled deeply, then looked at his new project. Excitement coursed through him at the possibilities. He could see the finished bike in his mind and knew he was going to love cruising on her, the first chance he got.

G race Murphy pulled her dog, Chiefy's, leash from the hook it was hanging on. Chiefy knew there was a walk in store, and immediately began to jump and whine in excitement.

Grace laughed, "I know girl, let's go, shall we?"

Attaching Chiefy's leash to her collar, she giggled as Chiefy's excitement poured over her. They exited their new little place across the road from the beach and began their walk down Sunset Beach Road. As Chiefy sniffed the ground, finding the perfect place to do her business, Grace looked toward the water and the bungalows on the beach. She had purposely bought across from the beach because she had the view, but the price was significantly lower because she wasn't on the beach. And, she had a public access path to the water from her place, so when she finally had her remodeling finished and could rent out her bungalows, short-term tenants could simply walk across the road and access the beach. Win-win as far as she was concerned.

Chiefy squatted and only tinkled, marking her territory in dog speak. Grace patiently waited and smiled as a group of young people began splashing each other on the sandbar. Her heart felt a little heavy as she watched. Those days for her were gone. Playful youth. No cares. No worries. She almost couldn't remember having a carefree life.

Chiefy finished her business then stopped and looked as one of the girls on the sandbar squealed. Chiefy let out a muffled bark and Grace laughed. "It's not your job to protect them, Chiefy."

She continued walking and Chiefy hesitantly followed along. Just past Sarge's Sandbar, the road curved to the right and away from the beach. The giggles of the folks in the water faded and the vehicles on Main Street took up the distraction. She led Chiefy to the right once again and onto Main Street. The loud boom of firecrackers filled the air and Chiefy barked. Grace shook her head. Her brother, rest his soul, would have had a monster PTSD attack at the sudden and unexpected crack filling the air. She'd never let off another firecracker after he came home from the service. His mind and body never recovered.

Swallowing the sadness that filled her throat, she sucked in a deep breath and picked up her pace. She passed the bookkeeping office, and Bodie's Gas Station. That's all the sign in the window said, *Bookkeeping*. Next to the gas station was a little garage, which had a peeling white sign with blue letters that said, *Garage*. She chuckled because it seemed no one here thought it was necessary to name their businesses anything but what they were, except for Bodie and Sarge.

Her eyes landed on a man in front of the garage, kneeling in front of an old motorcycle. She watched him because he was on his knees, his head down, his hands on his knees and he shook profusely. Images of her brother filled her mind. She recognized PTSD anytime, anywhere. Chiefy did too and she pulled Grace across the street toward the man.

Grace tugged on Chiefy's leash, not wanting to startle the man, but Chiefy was insistent in getting to him. Chiefy tugged and pulled until they reached him. She then slowly approached and laid down on the pavement next to the man, and rested her chin on his leg. Grace watched as her heart swelled for this smart, beautiful, and protective pet she'd inherited from her brother upon his death. Owning a German Shepherd hadn't been part of her single life plan, but here she was with Chiefy and immensely happy for it.

The man slowly lifted his left hand and patted Chiefy on the head, then smoothed his hand down her neck and rested it on her upper back. Grace watched for a few minutes, to be sure all was safe for Chiefy, then hurried inside the station. An old man peered around the open hood of a car, "Can I help you?"

"Yes. I need a bottle of water. Do you have one I can buy?"

He chuckled, then slowly stood and stepped around the vehicle wiping his hands on a rag. "I don't sell..."

She cut him off. "It's for him," she interrupted. Lowering her voice she whispered, "I think he's having a PTSD episode. Likely from the firecrackers that just fired off."

The old man peered outside at the kneeling man and nodded. He opened an old cooler in the back of the shop and pulled a bottle of water from inside. "Take it to him. I don't sell them here, but he can have mine."

Grace nodded, then slowly approached the still,

kneeling man. His hand had begun to pet Chiefy and Chiefy's tail began to slowly wag.

Grace twisted the cap on the bottle of water to loosen it, then held it down to the man. "Please take a drink of water to wet your throat. It will help."

The man's shoulders expanded as he took a deep breath and slowly his head rose. His deep brown eyes held so much in them. Pain. Embarrassment. Sorrow. His jaw clenched tightly and she shook the bottle slowly to entice him.

He reached up and took the water from her, their fingers brushing slightly. "Thanks." His raspy voice croaked out.

"You're welcome." Grace sat on the other side of Chiefy and patted her sweet pup. She whispered, "You're a good girl, Chiefy."

Taking a good long pull from the water bottle, the man then lowered it, replaced the cap, and nodded slowly. "She is a good girl. How did she know to do that?"

"Before me, Chiefy lived with my brother. He had severe PTSD. She was trained to help him with his attacks. She saw you from across the street and dragged me over here to help you. She's special in that way. She wants to help. Loves it. And the treats that go along with it."

The man chuckled. "Of course, the treats get attention."

Chiefy's ears perked up at treats and Grace reached into the little zippered pouch at her waist, for a liver treat for Chief. "Here you go, girl. You earned it."

The man took a deep breath and let it out slowly. "Thank you. I'm terribly embarrassed, but grateful you and Chiefy happened upon me. That one came out of the blue."

Grace nodded. "Likely those fireworks that were let off. They'd hit my brother the hardest."

He nodded slowly. "Yeah."

"My name is Grace Murphy. This is Chiefy, of course."

"My name is Sid Hoffman."

"It's nice to meet you, Sid. Are you working on this bike?"

For the first time she noticed the tools laying on the ground between his knees and the bike.

"Yeah. It's a project. I thought it would help me with..." He motioned to his body. "This."

She couldn't help but smile at him. "It's not you. I completely understand PTSD. So does this girl here." She added petting Chiefy. "You've likely been through something very traumatic and it's understandable it can affect you this way. I don't judge you for it. I admire you looking for something to help yourself. A project like this is perfect. Though, it sure looks like a big project."

Sid chuckled and for the first time, she noticed him as a man. He was handsome. Truly handsome. His deep dark brown eyes held all the emotions of his past, but his smile, was pure sexiness. His shoulders were broad, and his belly a bit soft, but he was still fit. Hell, who was she to judge, she had a soft belly and her butt had filled in more than her jeans cared. But at fifty years old, she was still in pretty decent shape. In her opinion at least.

"It'll be worth it if I can get her to work."

Grace smiled at him and nodded. "That it will."

She stood. "Well, Sid Hoffman, Chiefy and I will leave you to your project if you're alright."

"Thank you. I'm fine. I'm sorry to have interrupted your walk."

Grace chuckled. "Always happy to help a fellow veteran."

His eyes rounded. "You're a veteran?"

"Yes, sir. Army."

"Me too."

"We have that in common too, then."

His smile was yummy. "That we do. I hope to see you around. Do you live here?"

She took a deep breath. "I just bought two little bungalows across from the beach. They both need a lot of work, but they'll come along. My plan is to be in the short-term rental business if I can get the first one finished."

"That's a great location for short-term rentals. Right now, I'm living in one of Sarge's beach bungalows."

"Is that Sarge from Sarge's Sandbar?"

"One and the same. He's a friend from the service."

Grace smiled. "Then I'll make sure to frequent his establishment. I like to help out fellow veterans."

3

S id watched Grace and Chiefy saunter down the sidewalk together. Chiefy's tail wagged and she glanced up at Grace often. They had a bond for sure.

Grace was a pretty woman. A few soft lines around her gorgeous blue eyes were sexy. Her long dark hair framed her face nicely.

He shook his head and took a deep breath. He'd promised himself after his divorce, that he wouldn't bring another person into his sphere who had to deal with this bullshit PTSD that seemed to creep up on him without notice. He was lucky, he'd never been violent during an attack, but hearing the horror stories of those who had, kept him clear of entanglements.

"You okay, son?" Cooper's gravelly voice sounded from a few steps away.

Sid turned to look at the old man, whose deep worry lines seemed more prevalent now. "Yeah. I'm fine. Thank you."

Cooper nodded but stared for a few moments longer

and Sid's stomach twisted. "I'm not violent. My body just shakes, and I seem to freeze up."

Cooper shook his head. "I'm not worried you're violent. I'm worried you aren't taking care of yourself. You need to pack a lunch to come here and work, and you'll need to bring several bottles of water to stay hydrated. Especially working out here in the sun."

"Yes, sir. I'll do that."

"I believe I told you, Coop or Cooper. You don't need to call me sir."

"Yes, sir...Okay, Coop."

"That's more like it."

Without another word Coop shuffled into the garage. Sid watched him for a few minutes then chuckled. Coop's walk was much less appealing than Grace's. He could watch Grace walk away all day. He'd be mindful not to tell her that. If he saw her again, that is.

He picked up his wrench and continued to remove the parts he could get off easily. He then moved into the garage and asked Coop, "You have something I can put small parts and nuts and bolts in, so I don't lose them? I also need something I can soak parts in."

Coop picked his cap off his head, scratched his scalp, then reset his cap. "I have one of those little tin pans over in that corner..." He pointed across the garage. "And there's a parts soaker below it."

Sid ambled in the direction of both things and dug around in the mess. Maybe once he finished with the motorcycle, he'd come in here and clean and organize. This place needed some good old elbow grease and military organization.

Finding the tin pan, he blew dust out of it and bent to

find the parts soaker. A bunch of miscellaneous junk had been stacked on top of it, but he found it.

Pulling the parts soaker out, he saw it would need a cleaning before he'd soak anything in it. If this is how it would be, he'd be here all month trying to get that old Knucklehead running.

He began gathering supplies to clean the parts soaker and set to work. Two hours later he'd finished cleaning the soaker, filled it with oil to give these old parts a good oil bath, and started carting parts he'd removed into the garage for their bath.

Coop looked at his watch. "So, I'm about ready to head home."

Sid glanced at his watch. "It's only three o'clock."

"Yeah. I need a nap." He reached into his pocket and pulled out some keys. "Lock up when you leave."

"You trust me to be here alone?"

Cooper laughed. "What are you going to steal? It would take you four hours to find anything worth taking. My tools are good but they're old. I don't keep money here. I don't have vending machines. I have someone else's vehicle that still doesn't work and a few miscellaneous parts and pieces. If that's your big take, you can have it."

Coop tossed the keys into the air and Sid caught them in his right hand. Coop stared at him for a few moments, then nodded. "See you tomorrow, Sid."

"See you tomorrow, Coop."

The old man shuffled out to an old pickup truck. It took him some time to finally get himself inside then he waved and started the old truck up. It sounded great. It was a sleeper for sure. Didn't look like much, but it ran like a top. Mechanics did shit like that.

He chuckled and finished adding parts to the oil bath.

He spent some time sweeping the floor of the garage. He put some tools away, tossed old rags into the garbage, and hung up larger tools that belonged on the wall. He didn't do everything he wanted, but it felt good.

He took a deep breath and looked around the little garage. It felt real good. He felt good.

Sid walked into the little front reception area and locked the door. He pulled the chain on the open sign to turn it off, then sauntered into the garage area. He closed the two overhead doors, then stepped out of the service door between the garage doors and the reception area. Pulling the keys from his pocket, he locked the door. As he walked away from the Garage, he stopped on the sidewalk and looked at it once more. A grin spread on his face, and he found a new stride in his step as he moved down Main Street toward his little bungalow. Despite the middle part of the day when he had his PTSD attack, he managed it, with help, and continued on with his day. He'd never done that before. In the past, he'd have gone home and crawled in bed for the rest of the day. Most of the time anyway. They drained him.

Maybe this little town had healing powers after all. That's what Sarge had said about it.

4

G race and Chiefy finished their walk with a skip in their step. Yes, it seemed Chiefy felt pretty danged good about their day too. They helped someone today and it felt damned good.

Hanging Chiefy's leash on the hook by the door, Grace turned around and she began digging into her work. Today she was going to tile the wall above the bathtub. Heaving out a deep breath, Grace entered the bathroom and looked at the mess. She was so sick of living in a construction zone. But, really, what could she do? This was the plan and she needed to save her money right now for the projects, not lavish digs. Once she had this place finished, she'd move next door and work on that one. She could live over there for the time being, but this was better than that place, sadly. These cute little bungalows had been left to their own devices for years now. Which was surprising in this location.

Anyway, she'd had the exterminator over there a couple of times now, and she felt leaving it closed up was better than trying to live in it, in case there were still bugs living about. Such was life in Florida. At least that's what she'd been told. So, now, she added the quarterly pesticide treatments to her budget, and she felt it was well worth it, if not a little gross.

Heaving out a deep breath, Grace opened the five-gallon pail of premixed thin set and set the lid in the kitchen. She then opened the box of tile. Admiring them for a few moments, she smiled. Beachy blue subway tile was going to look fantastic in here. She'd marked her lines yesterday, so she was ready to begin.

Grabbing her trowel, she smeared a large swath of thin set onto the wall, then moved it around in small sections. Adding her tile to the thin set she worked meticulously to get the first wall completed.

Chiefy whined and Grace looked at her watch. It had been a couple of hours. It was time to let her play in the water. This was their routine. Sit on the front porch in the morning and watch the water while Grace had her two cups of coffee. Then go for a walk. Then work for a while and go for a walk after lunch. Then work. But in the evening, Chiefy got to run in the water and look for things left behind. She just loved ducking her head into the water and coming up with weird things. A piece of carpet. An old can. A discarded water bottle. Grace always brought a garbage bag with her and considered it their community service in keeping the water clean.

"Okay, girl. Hang on."

She washed her hands, looked at her clothing and decided to go for it. Thin set smudges and dust were all over her, but she'd been working, and she'd wear these clothes until her shower tonight. Luckily, she had two bathrooms here.

She dried her hands on a towel, then pulled Chiefy's

leash from the hook by the door. That got her excited. Running back to the kitchen, she pulled a garbage bag from the drawer and met Chiefy at the door. She attached the leash to Chiefy's collar and stepped outside.

Before crossing the road she looked both ways, then they hurried across. As soon as they were on the beach, Chiefy began tugging hard on the leash. Grace giggled at her enthusiasm. As soon as they were within a couple of feet, she unhooked the leash and let Chiefy run to the water. Sand kicked up behind her feet she ran so fast, and the splash she made when she dove into the water was huge. Grace laughed and neared the water waiting for Chiefy to come up with a treasure.

It didn't take Chiefy long to surface with a paper cup in her mouth, she dropped it on the beach and dove in for more. Grace picked it up and put it in the garbage bag, always with an eye on the water where Chiefy went in. She surfaced again with a piece of floor mat from a car. She dropped it and repeated. This would go on for the next half hour until she got tired of diving in.

She looked so happy when she surfaced. She always got a "good girl" and then took off again.

Chiefy surfaced with a glass bottle which looked like it had been for orange juice or something. Grace grimaced that glass was in the water, but Chiefy dropped it in front of her. "Good girl, Chiefy."

This time instead of jumping in the water, Chiefy took off running down the beach. Grace called, "Chiefy, here." Which normally brought her well-behaved girl right back. Except for this time.

Grace looked ahead to where Chiefy was running and saw Sid walking on the beach toward a bungalow. She remembered he'd said he lived in one. Sid, for his part, dropped to his knees and waited for Chiefy to come to him. Grace hurried toward Chiefy and Sid.

When she neared, she heard Sid laughing and Chiefy was licking his face. She stopped in her tracks as she watched them together. Her heart swelled so much it hurt. Sid pet her fur, and laughed as he was completely slobbered on. Then Chiefy laid down and rolled onto her back to get a belly rub. Sid complied, the smile on his face completely spellbinding.

Grace slowly approached, unsure if she should interrupt this moment. Sid looked up at her, the smile on his face intoxicating. "She's sure a friendly girl."

Grace smiled. "Usually not like this. Normally she listens so well. But, she beat a path to you like I've never seen before."

Sid's cheeks turned pink. He glanced at Chiefy, still enjoying a belly rub. "So you like damaged people, Chiefy?"

Grace felt heat climb up her chest. "You're not damaged."

Sid's eyes met hers. He stared for a while, then nodded, but said nothing.

5

S id stared for a long time at Grace. Emotion clogged his throat, and he wasn't sure if sound would come out if he said anything in response to her. He felt damaged. He came home from the Army damaged. His ex-wife couldn't deal with him and left. He'd kicked around trying to 'find' himself as the younger generation said. He'd made money over that time. He was absolutely kick-ass when it came to fixing things. But the garages in the larger cities were all about time and money. 'We billed this job out as two-hours. Don't go over.' Meaning, he had to do a half-assed job on it because the garage wanted another car in that spot in two hours. He hated it.

Then, he'd move to another place. It always seemed to be more of the same.

Grace's lips parted in a soft smile, and she cocked her head. "You're not damaged, Sid. You're dealing with something many don't have to deal with or even understand. That doesn't make you damaged."

He swallowed. "What does it make me then?"

"Unique. Different in how you handle things and do things. But, then again, aren't we all different?"

Sid chuckled. "I suppose we are."

Chiefy stood up and shook. Sand and water flew through the air. Sid jumped up and laughed. Grace backed away laughing.

"I'm sorry she got you all dirty." Grace chuckled.

He looked at her clothing and saw she'd been working today. "She got you too."

Grace shook her head. "I was already dirty. Today was a tiling day."

"Tiling. What are you tiling?"

"One of the bathrooms. I only have one wall finished. I'll finish one of the other two tonight and the other one tomorrow. Then, on to another task."

"Are you doing all the work on your own?"

She nodded. "As much as I can do. Of course, plumbing and electrical will need to be done by professionals."

"Do you have a lot of that work to do?"

"Not too much. Mostly, I'm hoping to only have to do cosmetic stuff. Painting, flooring, tiling the walls in the bathroom and back splash in the kitchen. Stuff like that. I can hang new light fixtures and so far, I haven't had to have wiring or plumbing work done. Fingers crossed it stays that way."

Sid watched Grace as she explained her work. Her cheeks turned pink and her hands moved faster. She was worried or embarrassed.

"What's your story, Grace Murphy?"

She stopped talking and stared at him. "What?"

"Why are you here. Alone. Working on these little bungalows on your own?"

Her fingers tucked her hair behind her ears and she swallowed. "I'm divorced. I came here to get completely away from a man who beat me down verbally throughout our marriage. He told me I couldn't do anything on my own. He told me I'd never make it without him. So, I'm here to prove him wrong. I've always known I could do this. Own a business. Manage rentals. Live on my own."

She ended her sentence with a nod and a swallow as if to punctuate her determination.

He smiled at her. "You'll do a terrific job."

"What makes you think so?"

He chuckled. "Determination. The way you take care of Chiefy shows me you have your heart in the right place. I don't think you can go wrong with all that."

He smiled at her, his eyes stared into hers. Her lips parted slightly and her tongue jutted out and swiped along her bottom lip. She pursed her lips together and inhaled a deep breath. "Thank you."

"Does that make you nervous?"

She chuckled. "I umm..." She sucked in a deep breath. "I'm not used to a man complimenting me. I'm not sure what I should do."

He leaned forward so their eyes were level. He smiled and softly replied. "Say thank you."

Her cheeks turned an adorable pink. "Thank you."

"There. That's all settled." He glanced down at Chiefy who had decided their conversation was boring and laid down on her side. He laughed. "I think we've bored her."

Grace laughed and it was adorable. She had the cutest little dimples. And, that smile of hers was like the sun shining high in the sky. His heartbeat thumped in his chest.

"She's tired from all the diving and garbage cleanup."

She held up the garbage bag. "She dives in and comes up with random stuff."

He laughed as he looked at Chiefy's tail. It thumped a few times as if she knew they were talking about her.

Moving his gaze to Grace he sucked in a deep breath. "I think we're a lot alike, Grace. We've both been through a lot in our life. We're both trying to move on from that. We're both new in town."

Grace's lips turned up in a soft smile. "I guess we are."

"Well, I better go clean up. Thanks again for helping me today. I do appreciate it. I'll be at the garage working on that bike for a couple of weeks. Please feel free to stop by if you see me while you're out walking."

"Thank you. We'll stop in and say hi. Chiefy would love that."

Sid grinned. "I'd love it too."

Her cheeks turned a rosy pink, her eyes locked on his and they stared at each other. Chiefy whined, and Grace nodded once, then addressed her pup. "Let's go girl."

She clipped Chiefy's leash onto her collar and as they began walking toward the road, Grace looked back once. The beguiling smile on her face was the memory he'd have with him all night. Likely many nights. And there was nothing wrong with that.

6

race stepped into her bathroom to begin work for today. She'd finished one of the smaller walls last night, after returning from her walk with Chiefy. She hummed the entire time, which surprised her when she thought on it now.

Beach life agreed with her. The weather was warm here. The water lapping outside as she drank her coffee in the morning, was like a balm. And, she met a new friend. Sid was handsome. And there was something about him that called to her. He seemed lonely, and there were so many times she felt lonely too.

Blowing out a breath, she decided to change her train of thought so she didn't get depressed. Look at what she was doing here. The tile was coming out beautifully and she couldn't wait to see the finished room. The only way to do that was to get at it.

She opened the new box of tile and removed the lid from the thin set bucket. She swathed a section of the wall with thin set and placed the first section of tile. She continued on in a methodical manner until she had the entire wall finished. Chiefy whined and she glanced at her watch. Two hours. She'd be painting next and remembered she needed some paintable caulk.

Washing her hands in the kitchen sink, she placed her over-the-body bag on, then grabbed Chiefy's leash by the door. "Come on girl. We have to go to William's Hardware store for caulk."

Chiefy didn't care of course, but Grace spoke to her a lot as if she did. Just before stepping outside, Grace looked at Chiefy, "Hang on, girl." She ran back to her bedroom, looked at her hair in the mirror and wiped some dust off her face. Her clothes had some dust on them from her work, but she'd brush that off outside. She picked her lip gloss off the dresser and applied it to her lips. One more glance and she went back to Chiefy, who'd begun pacing back and forth in front of the door.

"Sorry girl. I know you have to go." She picked up Chiefy's leash and opened the door.

They walked only a few steps when Chiefy had to pee. While she waited for her to finish her business, Grace bushed the dust off her clothing.

She looked over to the beach at a group of young people playing in the sandbar. She missed those days. She missed her old body too. She'd never wear a bikini these days. She'd gotten a bit soft. It was a one-piece-only time of her life.

Swallowing the bit of sadness that brought, she started walking as Chiefy finished her job.

A light breeze blew her hair back and it felt good on her skin. The breeze was warm, and it brought the aroma of salt water and blooming azaleas. A great combination.

They turned right with the road and then right on Main Street. She glanced across the street and down past the gas station to the garage where Sid worked. A group of about four bikers were at the garage. They looked like a rough bunch with their club colors and tattoos. She couldn't see Sid anywhere, but saw a man stalk out of the garage and motion for them to get on their bikes. He angrily looked back into the garage, climbed on his bike and they sped away.

Warning bells went off in Grace's head. A confrontation could send Sid into another attack. She hurried down the street as three of the bikers blew past her. The fourth pulled his bike in front of the gas station and on her side of the street. He parked in a way that he could see the Garage and that made her worry a bit more. She stepped off the sidewalk and crossed the street, not walking past the biker. Stupid, she thought to herself. There was no indication he'd harm her or Chiefy, but she didn't like the posture and demeanor of them as they stood in the Garage parking area.

She tried not looking his way as they passed, then Chiefy recognized where they were and began tugging on her leash. Grace moved into the Garage parking area and neared the open garage door. Chiefy tugged hard on her leash and Grace let her go. She ran into the garage and to the back wall. Grace stepped into the garage but remained close to the door.

Sid stood in front of a toolbox, leaning back against it. His eyes were closed and he was practicing even breathing. Chiefy sidled up to him and pressed her body against Sid. Sid's hand reached down and rested on Chiefy's head. Grace's eyes filled with tears as she watched her pup, so eager to help.

Swiping her eyes to wick the moisture away, she took a deep breath and let it out slowly.

Sid opened his eyes and immediately locked on hers.

"I won't hurt you."

Grace smiled. "I don't think you will. I'm giving you space."

Sid stood taller, and patted Chiefy's head. "Chiefy doesn't care about personal space."

Grace laughed. "She was trained to be an active support system. I was trained to support it by not hovering."

Sid swallowed deeply. She watched his Adam's apple bob up and down. He drew in a deep breath and let it out slowly then stepped closer to her. She took two steps forward and they met inside the garage.

Sid's voice was gravelly and low. "Thank you. You must be my guardian angel. You seem to come when I need you."

Chiefy whined. Sid chuckled. "And you too, Chiefy." He pet her vigorously and her tail wagged happily.

Grace smiled as she watched them. "Is everything alright with those bikers?"

Sid's Adam's apple bobbed again. "For the time being."

"What did they want?"

"They wanted me to be their club mechanic."

"Oh." She stared into his eyes. Those deep brown orbs were hard to look away from.

"I said no."

"I figured. It didn't look like a happy ending."

"No."

It was her turn to swallow. She liked being near him. This close to him. His body was bigger than hers. He was taller but maybe only a foot or so. His broad shoulders were still muscular, but his belly was slightly soft in the middle. Just like hers.

"Will you be alright? I see one of them watching the Garage now."

He inhaled deeply. "I'll be alright. What brings you around today?"

"We have to go to the hardware store for paintable caulk."

He chuckled. "You want a ride?"

"No, the walk will do us good. It tires her out so I can work for a while without her needing to be played with. Then, later tonight I'll let her dive into the water for treasures."

"Be careful." His voice was low. He pulled his phone from his back pocket. "What's your number? I'll text you so you have my number in case you need help."

"Why would I need help?"

"I said, just in case." He smiled and she was mesmerized.

7

Grace smiled as she told him her phone number. He tapped the numbers with his fingers as she gave them. He added her as a contact, then pressed the call button and put his phone to his ear.

Grace fished her phone from the little bag she carried around her shoulder and answered. "Hello, this is Grace Murphy."

Sid chuckled. "Nice to hear your voice, Grace Murphy. This is Sid Hoffman."

She giggled and he loved watching her happiness. Chiefy came over and sat beside Grace. Without effort, Grace patted Chiefy's head.

"Well, hello, Sid. What's new with you today?"

Grace's cheeks were an adorable pink. Her hair was slightly windblown, and her lips were shiny.

"Aww, just the usual. A run in with a local biker gang. A visit from a beautiful girl and her gorgeous owner. You know, a regular day."

Grace's smile grew. Her blue eyes sparkled as they

bantered, and he wanted to lean in and kiss her so bad his lips tingled.

"Wow, that sounds like a rather interesting day. Are all of your days are like that? This is the happening place to be then."

Sid chuckled. "That's what I hear. Stop by, anytime, every day. I'd love to see you."

She blushed again, dropped her eyes to the ground and her feet shifted. He remembered her comment yesterday about not being complimented by a man, and he thought she should be complimented every day. She was a good person. She was so beautiful. Resourceful and self-sufficient. Who could not want to watch this woman blossom?

He reached out and lifted her chin with his fingers. He saw her swallow and his heart squeezed. His thumb brushed her chin softly and their eyes met. The blue of the Caribbean Ocean is what he stared at. He leaned in slightly, mostly to give her the chance to back away. She didn't.

His head dropped down and he moved in closer. Closer still. Until their lips met. He kissed her lips softly and briefly. Pulling back slightly he waited, then she moved in and kissed him back.

Chuckling reached his ears as Coop waddled into the garage. Sid grinned but Grace's embarrassment was visible. Her face and ears turned a bright red. "Coop, have you met Grace Murphy and Chiefy?"

"Not formally, until now." Coop shuffled to them and held his hand out to Grace.

She placed her hand in his and shook. Coop chuckled and glanced down at Chiefy. "This is the girl who helped you out yesterday. Or should I say, girls?"

Chiefy's tail wagged and Coop leaned forward slightly to pat her on the head. "Chiefy. What kind of a name is that for a girl?"

Grace chuckled. "My brother named her after his friend, Chiefy. He was the leader of their ball team in the military. It started out as a joke that he was the chief ball organizer. Then it was shortened to Chief. He passed away a few years ago and when my brother got this girl here, he named her Chiefy in honor of his friend."

"Well, that's real nice now. She looks like a great honorarium for a good friend."

Grace smiled as she looked at Chiefy. "Yes, she is for sure."

Coop looked up at him and grinned. "Well, I'll leave you all to it then. I've got to finish up this old truck's brakes before the owner comes to collect it." He motioned toward the truck up on the hoist.

Grace smiled and nodded. "It was nice to formally meet you, Coop."

The old man nodded and grinned. His gray hair still stood out from his scalp in a wild array of waves and directions. "It's nice meeting you ladies too."

Coop nodded, turned and grinned at him, then shuffled to the old truck up on the hoist.

Grace turned toward the door and Sid followed alongside her. As they reached the door, he noticed the biker still watching the Garage. Grace noticed too.

She inhaled a deep breath. "Are you going to be alright, Sid?"

He swallowed the emotion that rose in his throat. When was the last time someone truly cared about him in this way? It had been entirely too long for sure.

"I'll be alright, sweetheart. You ladies go on down to

William's and get your stuff. If he's still there when you come past, stop in and I'll get you home safely."

"Okay. We'll be alright."

She took a couple of steps then turned back to him. "Thank you."

He chuckled. "For what?"

"For caring. For complimenting me. But, mostly, for caring."

Emotion clogged his throat and his vision wavered as moisture gathered in his eyes. He took a deep breath to let his body adjust to the flood of feelings that raced through him. "You're very welcome, Grace. I should thank you for the same thing. Thank you for caring, lady."

She smiled as their eyes locked. Chiefy whined and Grace shrugged. "Gotta go."

He swallowed the lump in his throat and nodded but he couldn't say anything just now. He watched Grace and Chiefy hurry toward the sidewalk, then turn left to head to William's. As he turned, his eyes skimmed past the biker still watching the Garage. He moved to the toolbox and pulled a couple of wrenches from the drawer, then went outside to finish putting the old Knucklehead's parts back on after they'd soaked in an oil bath last night.

He kept a side-eye on the biker to make sure he didn't follow Grace and told himself it didn't matter that he sat here all day watching the Garage. What did he think he was going to see anyway? Or, perhaps it was a scare tactic. Whatever. If the biker only knew the things he'd had to do in his life in the military, he'd realize not much scared him. Certainly not someone staring at him.

He wrestled a couple of parts back on, worked over some of the parts to get them on using a rubber mallet, and clapped when the final part had been man-handled onto the old bike.

He glanced toward the Garage, then chuckled as he straddled the old ripped and rusted seat pan. That and the paint on the old girl would be the last thing he worked on. Right now he wanted to get her started, then he'd work on new tires, brakes, the chain, and other components to make her actually rideable.

Turning the gas petcock to on, he turned the choke to full choke. He primed the motor and filled it with gas, turned the key on and kicked the kick-starter a few times. She rumbled at first, sputtered a bit, then she started. He rolled the throttle a couple of times and Coop stepped out of the garage laughing and clapping his hands.

"Well done, Sid. Well, done." The old man praised.

Sid's heart swelled with pride. She had a lot of work to be done on her, but he'd gotten it started! He couldn't wait to tell Grace he'd gotten this old girl started. He glanced down the street and didn't see her coming, and a sadness washed over him. He wanted to share this with her. Coop came to stand a few feet away from him, the biggest smile on his face Sid had seen to date.

Then, he saw her. Grace. She had started to jog toward him, Chiefy running alongside her. Grace's smile was wide, her face an absolute delight. She and Chiefy stopped next to Coop and Grace clapped her hands. Chiefy wasn't as excited and barked at the noise.

Oh, the look on his face at his accomplishment. He was a sexy man. He looked good in a garage, surrounded by tools and bikes and cars. He seemed relaxed here. And working with his hands seemed to come second nature. The PTSD aside. There would always be things that could trigger him no matter where he was. But, last night on the beach, while they had a nice chat, he seemed a bit stiff. When she looked at him now, his body showed a relaxed state she hadn't noticed yet.

She clapped her hands and smiled so big her cheeks hurt. He twisted the throttle a couple of times and the bike sputtered slightly. When it sputtered and coughed, then stopped, he grinned and moved off the bike.

"She still needs some work, but I couldn't wait to get her started."

She giggled. "It's awesome. Congratulations."

Coop nodded and slapped him on the back. "You've got a knack, I'll say that, miracle man."

His cheeks turned an adorable pink. He nodded, "Thank you."

He pulled a rag from his back pocket and wiped his hands on it.

He glanced down the street briefly then looked into her eyes. "You want me to take you home in the truck?"

Her eyes slid to the biker still watching them. "No. I'll be fine. I have Chiefy and not far to go. I don't want to take you away from your work."

"Call me if something happens. Actually, pull your phone out and have it ready just in case."

"Okay." She pulled her phone from her little shoulder bag. She leaned down to Chiefy and rubbed her neck. "Ready to go, girl?"

Chiefy stood and shook then her tail wagged vigorously. Grace giggled and looked at Sid.

He grinned and nodded. "You're so good with her."

"I love her."

He nodded and his eyes met hers. "Love makes everything so much better."

Her heart thumped so hard in her chest she wondered if he could hear it. "It does."

He whispered, "Be careful." Then he smiled. "Call me if you feel uneasy or need me to come over. I'll be right there."

"Thank you."

She sucked in a deep breath, then turned toward the sidewalk, Chiefy was right there with her. As a general rule, Chiefy walked on the inside of the sidewalk so she could sniff all the grasses, flowers, and anything else close by. But, just a few steps toward Sunset Beach Road and the biker who still sat astride his bike watching, Chiefy moved to the street side of the sidewalk and her head continued to turn toward the biker. Grace didn't look his way, but she did watch Chiefy's demeanor, which was all she needed.

As soon as they passed the biker and stopped at the stop sign to turn left onto Sunset Beach Road, she heard the motorcycle start up. Her heart raced and her stomach tightened. Chiefy growled low and deep.

She patted her head, "It's okay, girl."

Keeping her breathing even, Grace crossed the street, then turned down Sunset Beach Road. She stayed on the opposite side of the road from her house, thinking she'd duck into Sarge's Sandbar if the biker came close. Sid said Sarge was his friend. She instantly felt he'd help her if she needed it.

The motorcycle seemed to drive off in the opposite direction, based on the sound fading away. She wanted to turn and make sure he didn't stop at the Garage but she was afraid he'd see her and start to follow her. She didn't want him to know where she lived.

Her heart beat hard, her breathing came in spurts, and she began to sweat. Chiefy continued to look up at her. She was smart and could likely feel Grace's heightened fear. She didn't know why she feared him, but that's likely what he wanted and why he sat staring at the Garage for so long. Instill fear just for the fun of it.

She was now in front of Sarge's and didn't see or hear the biker, so she let herself relax slightly. She and Chiefy crossed the street, and she picked up her pace to get home as quickly as she could. Right now, the only thing she wanted was to get home.

The bag of caulk she carried swung as their pace picked up. Her house came into focus and excitement sped through her body. She smiled for no reason at all other than the safety of home was just ahead.

Chiefy seemed to sense it too as her pace picked up slightly. Grace kept in step with Chiefy and they were only two houses away when the sound of a motorcycle reached her ears. Her breathing increased and she started a slow jog, afraid to look back. Chiefy growled again but Grace only sped up.

She pulled her keys from her little purse and found the key she needed to minimize her time outside. The instant they stepped up on the little porch, Grace stuck the key in the lock and turned. The door opened and she and Chiefy hurried inside. She let go of the leash and hurried to twist the locks on the door. The one on the knob and the deadbolt. Leaning back against the door she allowed herself a moment to get her pulse to slow down.

Chiefy ran to her water dish for a long drink. The sound of the motorcycle grew louder then shut off. She closed her eyes and took a deep breath. Scooting to the window in the living room, she dropped the bag of caulk tubes onto the sofa, and peered out between the curtains and the window and there he sat. Same bike. Same biker. Same distance away. Not close enough she could call the police but still there. Watching.

She checked the locks on the doors. All good. Hurrying to the back door she checked the locks. Good again. Then, just for good measure, she checked the locks on all the windows.

Feeling as safe as she could be for now, she chided herself for being paranoid and filled Chiefy's dish with food. She picked up the bag of caulk and stepped into the bathroom where it'd be used first. She pulled out a tube from the bag and inserted it in her caulk gun, but her hands were shaking. Laying the caulk gun down, she moved out to the kitchen and poured herself a glass of iced tea.

She took a healthy drink of it, set the glass on the counter, and a loud knock on her door caused her to yelp. Chiefy began barking and Grace hurried to the living room door. She didn't have a peep hole and wished right now she did.

"Grace." Knock, knock. "Open up, it's Sid."

9

S id watched that biker. He moved past the Garage then slowly back again. When he kept going, a growing unease in his stomach had him watching. Sure enough, he could hear him down Sunset Beach Road, then stop.

The day prior, Sid found a foot path that ran through the alley across the street from the Garage, then across a private road, through a thicket of palm trees and between Grace's places. No need to go past the biker. Sid knocked on her door and heard her yelp inside.

"Grace." Knock, knock. "Open up, it's Sid."

His relief was immediate when he heard her twisting the locks. Her eyes were wide in fear when the door swung open. "Sid, you scared me." She stepped back to allow him room to come in.

Chiefy ran to him, her tail wildly swaying. Her excitement at seeing him made his heart warm.

"I'm sorry to do that to you, Grace." He leaned down and patted Chiefy. "I heard the biker drive down here and figured he was trying to scare you. I'm afraid he's focused on you because of me."

"How would I have anything to do with it?"

"He saw you come to the Garage after his group left. We chatted, he saw us talking. After I started the bike, you came back. So, he's likely thinking we're a couple. Which, unfortunately for you, caught his focus."

Grace nodded. She twisted the locks on the door and moved toward the kitchen area in the little open concept bungalow.

"The fact that you were scared tells me he's making you nervous."

"He is. Not gonna lie." She pulled a glass from a cupboard. "Would you like some iced tea?"

"That would be great."

He moved into the house a bit further. It was evident that construction projects were underway as there were tools, supplies, and other things laying around.

"What's the project of the day?" He asked.

She picked up the two freshly poured iced teas and handed him one. "The bathroom. I just finished tiling the walls. You wanna see?"

He chuckled. "I sure would."

Grace moved past him and turned right into the first room. She flipped on the light. "I'm letting the grout dry. I was going to caulk around the sink and trim boards, but ..." She bushed her hands on her hips, "my hands were shaking so I took a break."

He swallowed. He hated that she was scared. She didn't deserve this at all.

Taking in the room and what she'd completed, he smiled. The room looked nice. She was good at color choice and tiling. "You did this all yourself?"

Her smile was adorable. "I did."

"You've done a good job, Grace. Wow. Nice work."

Her cheeks tinted a nice bright pink. She twisted her fingers together in front of her. "Thank you."

He saw the paint can sitting on the floor. "What color are you going to paint this room?"

"Oh, it's a light blue. The same hue of the tile, but a lighter shade. I was going to caulk first, let it dry overnight, and paint tomorrow."

"That's a great idea. I don't mind caulking if you have something else to do."

She tilted her head up so their eyes met. "You don't have to come here and work."

"Didn't you say the sooner you get this place done the sooner you can make money with it?"

She chuckled. "I did."

"Well, I'm finished at the Garage for tonight, so let me help you. At the same time, I'll be here if the biker starts any trouble."

She visibly swallowed. "Okay."

"Good." He picked up the caulk gun and the utility knife on the bathroom counter. He snipped the end of the caulk tube off, then poked a hole into the tube. Turning the pin down on the caulk gun, he knelt on the floor and began caulking along the baseboards. He enjoyed this kind of work and he especially enjoyed doing it for someone who was so nice.

Grace stepped out of the bathroom, but Chiefy came in and licked his cheek once, then walked away. He chuckled and considered that her way of saying thank you.

He worked quietly until he'd finished the caulking around the baseboards and the door trim. Then he caulked around the new granite top on the sink.

He finished and moved into the living room, which was also open to the kitchen, to see Grace removing the cabinet doors from the cupboards.

"What are you doing in here?"

"I'm going to paint these a nice creamy white. I think it'll brighten the whole place up a bit."

He nodded. "I think you're right."

He picked up a screwdriver laying on the counter and started helping to remove the doors. "What are you going to do with the hardware?"

"I'm not sure. I was hoping to save it, but it looks old and dated."

"I'll bet if you soak it in vinegar, you'll see how clean it will get, and can decide then if you want to keep this hardware or not."

"Really? That's a great idea."

She pulled a glass bowl from the cupboard and poured vinegar into it while he removed the handles from the cabinet doors.

Chiefy began whining and Grace smiled at her. "Is it time to go clean the beach?"

Chiefy's tale wagged furiously and she jumped around. Grace giggled and he stopped what he was doing and prepared to leave. "How about, while Chiefy is cleaning up the beach, I go into Sarge's and order us some food. We can eat on the beach and relax a bit."

"That sounds really nice, Sid. But, I don't want to take you away from your fun."

Sid laughed out loud. "I don't have any fun, sweetheart. I've just been working and trying to figure out what I'm going to do with my life."

"You don't have a place to go home to?"

"No. Not really. I have a small condo I'm renting, back in Minnesota, but nothing really holding me there. It's where I grew up. My parents were there when I left the military, so I found a little place to be close to them. But they're both gone now, and I'm there alone."

"I'm sorry for your loss. Do you have siblings?"

Sid grinned. "One sister who lives in Montana."

"You don't think you'll go there and live, to be near her?"

He watched her eyes as she spoke. They were clear and incredibly pretty. Her lashes were thick without globs of mascara coating them.

"No. I've visited out there a few times, but it isn't for me. No reason in particular other than I don't get that sense of feeling comfortable there."

Grace nodded and pulled Chiefy's leash from the hook on the wall. She clipped it on Chiefy's collar and giggled as her pup jumped around. "Do you feel comfortable here?"

Nodding, he grinned. "Just today I was thinking how nice this town is and how I've come to enjoy it in the short three weeks I've been here. So, I guess, yes, I feel comfortable here."

The smile she bestowed on him was incredible. Her lips weren't shiny like they'd been earlier today, but they looked soft.

He licked his lips then bent down and kissed hers once more. Her hand wrapped around the back of his neck and he snaked his left arm around her waist and pulled her close. Her body fit his wonderfully. She was soft, like pulling a pillow close and hugging it.

He tested her lips with his tongue and when her lips parted to let him in, he didn't hesitate. The feel of his tongue sliding against hers sent electric waves through his body. The current sizzled through him at lightning speed.

Grace's right arm wrapped around his waist and her fingers splayed on his back. His body roared to life like a hungry bear waking from its winter sleep.

Then two things happened to break the spell. The roar of several motorcycles outside broke the relative silence of the house and Chiefy began barking loudly.

10

Her heart raced as Sid's lips touched hers. The beating increased again as Sid's arm wrapped around her. The feel of his body against hers felt so danged good. It was a new, welcome, but strange sensation. It had been literally years since this type of excitement coursed through her body. His warmth enveloped her and his strength made her feel safe.

When the motorcycles revved up though, his arm banded tighter around her, and she could feel his heartbeat against her chest. And the protectiveness he demonstrated toward her was dizzying. Hadn't she always dreamed of someone wanting to protect her without telling her how stupid she was. Or insecure or a baby? Always. She'd always dreamed of how lovely that would be.

His voice was a low growl when he stepped back. "Hang on for a minute while I check this out."

His tall frame moved to the window with ease. Pulling the curtains back slightly, he peered outside for a few moments then dropped the curtain into place.

"It looks as though they're at the Sandbar."

"Okay." She watched his eyes. They were incredible to look at. An enviable deep brown that reminded her of dark oak. There was a richness in them that made it difficult to look away.

His brows rose slightly. "So we have two options. We can go over as if nothing is going on. Jace won't tolerate any bullshit there. And, certainly not toward me. And, not toward you by extension. Or we can walk Chiefy in another direction."

Grace bit her bottom lip and squared her shoulders. She would not be a coward. "Chiefy just loves the water and she hasn't done anything wrong to be slighted her time to play."

"I agree with you. I simply wanted you to be comfortable."

She stepped back. "That biker today didn't do anything more than sit and stare. Scare tactic. I'd like to be cautious, but not be a scaredy cat about anything that isn't there."

She was nervous for sure. But, she had been a coward her entire adult life. When her ex said she couldn't do something and made her feel small. Inept. Helpless. She'd silently accepted it to avoid more backlash. She'd told herself when moving here that she'd never be helpless again. Those bikers were trying to scare them, and while they were kind of doing that, she wasn't going to give them the satisfaction. Plus, what would they possibly do in public?

Sid nodded once. "Okay, let's go then."

He stepped forward and opened the door for her and Chiefy. As they stepped onto her little patio area, she turned and locked the door with her key. Sid waited next to her, Chiefy pranced. It was difficult for her to contain her excitement and she didn't understand what was going on with the bikers.

As they walked across the front lawn, Sid took her hand in his, and they held hands across the road and the lawns in front of the little bungalows on the beach. His hand felt so good holding hers. His was roughened by work and strong.

He led her between two of the bungalows and pointed to the one on the right. "This is my bungalow for the time being."

"Boy, you have the best beach view."

He chuckled. "That I do. But, the down side is I hear all the beach activities. The music is nice, but as the patrons drink more, they get louder and that carries into my place."

Grace chuckled. "I hear that sometimes too. And, I'm slightly removed from where you are."

"Yeah." He turned his head and looked toward the Tiki Bar on the sand. "If I were on vacation here, it wouldn't be that bad. It adds to the vacation lifestyle."

"You are sort of on vacation, aren't you?"

Sid looked out at the water. "I suppose I am. But, for some reason, it feels like I'm now a resident here. I enjoy working at the Garage. I enjoy visiting with Jace and Quinn."

She smiled, "Tell me about them?"

He swallowed. "Quinn owns a construction company here in town. He's the reason Jace came here. Quinn was born and raised here. Jace had gotten out of the military and struggled with his PTSD. Quinn told him to come down for a bit and see if a change in scenery helped. Jace stopped in at the bar." He tilted his head toward the bar.

"He got a job as a bartender on his first day. He thought, 'What the hell?' and started tending bar. But, there were things he tried fixing up or changing and the old fella who owned it, didn't want all that *fancy stuff*, as he called it. Then, one day out of the blue, a couple of years later, the old fella walked in and told Jace he could buy the bar if he wanted. Jace didn't need to think about it long. He's been fixing it all up since that time. He said it's helped his PTSD a lot to have so much to do and think about."

Grace smiled. "That's great. He's found a way to channel it. Good for him."

"Yeah. Quinn has done a remarkable job too. He owns a construction company and he only hires veterans. He's so proud of that. Jace is leaning that way as well. It's harder for him though, it's not easy finding former military personnel who want to wait tables and tend bar. But, he only hires Quinn's company for work because of their friendship, but also Quinn's mission. Plus, Quinn is an excellent contractor."

Grace bent to release Chiefy's leash. She giggled as Chiefy ran into the water but when her eyes turned toward Sid's, she found him watching her.

Her cheeks burned almost instantly. Her throat dried and she swallowed to wet it. Sid grinned. "Tell me about your brother."

She inhaled a deep breath and glanced toward the water for Chiefy. She came bounding from the water with part of an old tennis shoe. Dropping it at Grace's feet, she waited for her "good girl" then bounded off again.

Grace laughed briefly as she watched her energetic pup. "My brother's name was Travis. He served in the Army. He was deployed to Iraq twice. He came home changed. He'd seen countless atrocities. He didn't want to talk about them. He refused help. He tried committing suicide twice before he finally accepted counseling. He got Chiefy. She helped him. But, he struggled so much. He took too many pills one night and didn't wake up again."

She swallowed the dark emotion that welled up in her. She remembered going to his house in the morning because he didn't answer his phone. Chiefy was howling inside and the sick dread that filled her took her a couple of years to erase.

"I'm sorry, Grace."

She sucked in a deep breath and let it out in a whoosh as Chiefy ran up to her with a soggy piece of cardboard.

She blinked away unshed tears. "Thank you. He saved me though. He couldn't save himself, but he saved me."

"How so?"

She bent to put the soggy cardboard at her feet into the garbage bag. "I knew then that I'd divorce. I wasn't going to stay in that toxic relationship anymore. I wasn't really living either, and Travis had told me that more than once. He worried about me as much as I worried about him."

Sid stood staring out at the water with her. The seconds ticked by, both of them lost in thought. Chiefy came running toward them, breaking the melancholy spell that had fallen over them. She shook her wet coat over them and they both jumped back and laughed. It felt good to laugh. It felt great to have someone to laugh with.

11

an two broken people make a whole? Since his divorce he'd avoided relationships. He brought too much to deal with into any relationship. But, dammit, he was drawn to Grace and wondered if she'd want a relationship with someone as broken as him.

"You're a good person, Grace." He absently offered.

Her face turned toward him once again. The sun dipping into the water shrouded her in a beautiful orange glow. Her eyes, those blue, blue eyes, against the warm orange glow, stood out to him. When she looked into his eyes, he felt...peace. He felt peaceful with her. She was a calm personality in a chaotic world.

"So are you, Sid." Her lips parted in a soft smile and his heart swelled.

He swallowed the lump that clogged his throat and focused on evening out his breathing.

"Do you ever think about being in a relationship again? After a bad relationship, sometimes, it's so hard to want another one."

He watched her throat move as she swallowed. Her

eyes stared into his for a long time and his stomach began twisting. He shouldn't have asked. It was weird. He'd just made it weird. If only he could turn back the clock a few minutes.

"I thought when I moved here that I'd live out my days building my business and watching the sun set into the water each night." He nodded and stepped back. She reached out and took his hand and squeezed his fingers. "Then I met an incredibly handsome man who is equal parts sweet and hurt. He loves my dog. He's a kickass mechanic and I find that each day I look forward to seeing more of him."

Did he...did he hear her correctly? It was his turn to swallow. Her lips parted into a sweet smile, and Chiefy bounded up to them, soaking wet, and dropped a dripping mess of an old carpet on his feet.

Grace laughed and jumped back. She bent and patted Chiefy on the head, "Good girl, Chiefy." Then picked up the drenched carpet piece, using just her thumb and forefinger to attempt to drop it into the garbage bag.

Sid laughed. He actually burst out laughing and his spirits lifted tenfold. She meant him.

He bent down and took that piece of carpet out of her hands. "You hold the bag open, I'll drop it in."

"Okay."

After his deposit, they both stood up and he pulled her into his arms. He stared down into her mesmerizing eyes for a few moments, then he bent his head and kissed her. Her arms wrapped around his waist and his arms wrapped around her shoulders and enclosed her into the safe, warm cocoon of his protection. He wanted to protect her for certain.

They were spattered once again with water as Chiefy shook herself off. They both started laughing.

He stepped back and saw this time Chiefy didn't have a soggy gift for them, so her cleaning efforts for today were over.

"Let's go get a table and order food for us and water for this girl, shall we?"

"Yes, please." She bent and clipped Chiefy's leash on.

He took her soft but strong hand in his. He liked the feel of holding her hand. She squeezed his and his heart beat a little faster.

He found them a table on the edge of the beach, where Chiefy wouldn't be in the way. Chiefy eagerly laid in the warm sand next to the table and he held a chair out for Grace. She sat with a sweet smile on her lips just as one of the waitstaff stopped by.

"Hey, folks. How can I help you?" She glanced at Sid, then grinned. "Hi, Sid, sorry I didn't recognize you right away."

"Hey there, Jan. This is Grace and Chiefy." He motioned to the sand.

"Oh, nice to meet you, Grace." She laughed. "And Chiefy."

"So, we'd like a bowl of water for Chiefy, please. Grace what would you like?"

"I'd love a rum punch."

"Oh, we make a good one here. Jace calls it the Sandbar Punch."

Grace smiled at Jan and he loved watching her interact with people. "Perfect."

Jan wrote it down then looked at him. "I'll take the same, please."

"Sounds good. I'll let Jace know you're out here."

"Thanks."

Jan hustled off and he reached across the table and laid his hand over Grace's.

"This is really nice." She grinned. "I haven't done this since I've been here. I've watched plenty of others sit here and eat a meal, but I'm not one to come to a place like this alone, so I've lived vicariously through them."

She turned her hand over and they locked fingers.

He grinned at her. "I usually eat at the bar. It's when Jace and I get the chance to chat about stuff."

"I heard my name."

He laughed as he turned toward his friend and pointed to a chair at the table.

"Jace Marriott, meet Grace Murphy. Grace, this is my friend Jace, bar owner extraordinaire, good friend, all around great guy."

Grace moved her hand from his and held her hand out to Jace. "It's nice to meet you Jace Marriott, bar owner extraordinaire, good friend, and all-around great guy."

Jace laughed. "I'm at a loss. Sid, you didn't describe Grace for me."

Sid chuckled. "Ah yes. Grace is a beautiful soul who also can fix up an entire house on her own and she's a fur mom to Chiefy here." He pointed to Chiefy who heard her name and jumped up.

"It's nice to meet you, Grace. And, Chiefy."

Chiefy moved around Grace and sniffed Jace hesitantly. Her tail wagged, then she laid back down.

Sid glanced at Jace. "Are the bikers behaving themselves?"

"Yes. Is that the group you texted me about?"

"Yes. One of them sat on his bike down from the Garage most of the afternoon, then followed Grace to her place..." He pointed across the road to Grace's. "Over there."

Jace's jaw tightened. "Well, don't be cowed by them and don't take any crap from them." Jace turned to Grace. "If Sid is at the Garage and they come close to your house, feel free to call me here. I'll come over and help out."

Grace smiled beautifully. "Thank you so much, Jace. I appreciate it."

12

race watched as Sid and Jace chatted. They were solid friends who shared unspeakable horrors of war. Both had suffered, still suffered, but were contributing members of society.

Jace turned to her, a smile on his face. "So, tell me about you, Grace. How much work do you have to do over at the house and then what will you do?"

"I own both of those houses." She pointed toward her twin bungalows. "I'm currently living in one and fixing it up. Then, I'll move to the second while I rent out the first. My plan is short-term rentals. I'd like a few more eventually so I can make enough to live on. I have a fair amount of work to do, but luckily, most of it is cosmetic. Painting, tiling, things like that."

Jace chuckled. "Short-term rentals are popular here. I have four of them myself. But, mine came with the bar, and right now I have a couple of friends living in them..." He grinned at Sid. "I'm also paying Quinn to fix up the other two. So, I'd say I have more going out than coming in. But, that will change soon."

"I know what you mean," she chuckled.

Sid grinned as they spoke and she enjoyed the fact that he didn't seem jealous or possessive. She'd had enough of that over the years.

Jace addressed Sid. "Tell me about the Garage. I heard through the grapevine you got the Knucklehead started."

Sid's smile was electric, his cheeks dimpled, and his eyes sparkled. "I did. It felt good. But she has a long way to go to be ride-ready."

Jace laughed. "I have no doubt you'll get her ride-ready."

The server came out with their drinks and Chiefy's water bowl and Jace nodded. "I gotta get back inside. Stop in when it's quiet, we'll have more time to chat." Jace stood. "Nice to meet you, Grace." He glanced over the table at Chiefy, "You too, Chiefy."

Chiefy's tail wagged twice, but she was tuckered out. She barely lifted her head.

Jace leaned in slightly, "I'm watching the bikers and I've got a friend who is the local detective here in town. If you have issues, I'll give her a call."

Sid grinned. "How good of a friend?"

Jace pointed a finger at his friend and chuckled. "A friend. That's it."

Jace started back toward the bar, stopping at tables and asking the patrons if they were happy with their meals and laughing with them as he went. Sid watched his friend and shook his head as he chuckled. "He's a natural at this."

"He sure seems to enjoy his business. That's the key though, isn't it?"

Sid nodded. "It is."

Suddenly the doors from the bar burst open and the

bikers came pouring out. There were many of them, perhaps ten. Chiefy jumped up and moved to sit between Grace and the bikers.

Grace smoothed Chiefy's neck hair. "It's okay girl. We're good."

Chiefy growled slightly. A low, warning growl.

Jace switched direction and stood before the bikers. "No bullshit out here. Got it."

"Fuck you, man. We're not doing anything wrong."

"Your posture and demeanor tell me you're looking for trouble. I'm just saying don't. I'll call the police faster than you can throw the first punch."

The first biker chuckled. It wasn't a happy chuckle, it was slow and menacing. He turned to his friends and a couple of them nodded.

Sid leaned forward. "Grace, call 911."

She pulled her phone from her little bag. It was made difficult by her shaking fingers. Between trying to keep Chiefy calm and herself calm, she felt slow as a turtle and clumsy.

Finally retrieving her phone, she tapped and held the number nine on her phone and held it to her ear.

"911 what's your emergency?"

"Hello. My name is Grace Murphy and my friend and I are at Sarge's Sandbar outside. There's a group of bikers here and it looks as though they're sporting for a fight. The owner is trying to talk them down, but the "F" bomb is being tossed around a lot and the group is advancing on the owner."

"We'll be right there. Can you stay on the line with me?"

"Ye...yes."

She turned her eyes to Sid's and nodded. She stared

into his eyes to make sure he wasn't going to have an episode, but he seemed just fine. He sucked in a deep breath and stood.

"Sid. No."

"I'm sorry ma'am, what's going on?"

"I'm speaking to my friend." Grace reached for Sid's hand, and he turned in her hand and squeezed her fingers.

"I have to help my brother. We stick together. Stay on the line with the police."

Chiefy growled a bit louder and Grace's breathing began to come in shallow spurts. "Are they on their way?" Her voice shook.

"Yes, ma'am."

"They need to hurry."

"Yes, Grace, I'm messaging them. You should be hearing sirens soon."

The sirens finally filled the air and Chiefy growled louder and let out a low muffled bark.

"Shh."

Grace watched Sid as he approached the group and stood alongside Jace. His shoulders were pulled back, his back was rigid, his hands at his sides, fingers balled into fists.

Another man stomped over to Sid and Jace and stood alongside Sid. Sid glanced briefly at the man, but they all stood facing the bikers.

Jace's voice raised, "Get out."

"We haven't done anything wrong."

"You're behaving in a threatening manner. I don't have to serve you. Get out."

Sirens grew louder and stopped out front and Grace's eyes filled with moisture. Her voice was shaky when she spoke to the 911 operator. "They're here. Thank goodness, they're here."

"I'll let you go then, Grace. Unless you want me to stay on the line."

"No." She gripped Chiefy's leash tighter as she began prowling toward Sid. "No, thank you."

She ended the call and set her phone on the table. She gripped Chiefy's leash with both hands and let out a shaky breath when police walked toward the group of men. Two officers began talking the situation down. Sid, Jace, and the third man stepped back at police request, but they didn't stop watching the action.

Grace's heartbeat felt as though she'd just run a marathon, her throat was dry, and her fingers, had they not been holding Chiefy's leash so tight, would be shaking like they were on a vibrating bed.

13

S id stood tall next to his brothers. The bond they'd formed while fighting a common enemy bonded them for life. He'd help them no matter the fight, and no matter the detriment to himself. He'd deal with any fallout later.

He'd be lying though, if he said he didn't feel relief sizzle through him when he heard the sirens. He'd schooled his face not to show any emotion, but the emotion that flooded through him was dizzying.

When Quinn joined them shoulder to shoulder, it felt like the old days. Only they weren't in uniform, and they didn't have weapons.

When the officers approached though, he was so grateful he sent up a silent prayer of thanks that hopefully this was all going to be resolved quickly. The real issue though, would be tomorrow if they stopped at the Garage again. He'd have to figure out how to keep them at bay and keep Coop safe.

And Grace. How would he keep her safe too? These assholes could come in the middle of the night to scare her. He wouldn't be there. She'd be alone and they'd likely know that.

The female officer moved toward Jace. "You good here, Jace?"

"Yes, ma'am. I'd like them to leave. And, I'd like them to not come back. This is a place of relaxation, play, good times, and camaraderie. They don't go with that vibe."

She grinned then glanced at both he and Quinn. "You gentlemen should go back to your tables, please."

Quinn nodded. "I just got here and don't have a table yet, so I can..."

Sid nudged him. "Come sit with Grace and I."

Quinn nodded and stepped back for him to lead the way. As they approached the table, Chiefy stood, her tail wagging furiously and Grace visibly inhaled a deep breath.

He bent and patted Chiefy's head and smoothed her fur. "Good girl."

He looked into Grace's eyes. "Thank you."

"Of course."

He moved his drink to sit next to Grace and offered his chair to Quinn. "Grace, this is my friend Quinn Kurtz."

"Hi, Quinn. You're the builder I've heard about."

"All good things I hope."

Grace chuckled. "All good."

Quinn let out a deep breath. "However, I'm at a loss. I haven't heard anything about you and your pup here."

Sid took Grace's hand on the table and turned his head to Quinn. "Grace is new in town. She's fixing up those bungalows across the road." He pointed. "They'll be short-term rentals for her."

Quinn chuckled and nodded. "That's a good business to be in in Blossom Springs. We have loads of tourists all the time. The weather is usually great. The fabulous sunsets make it popular, and the sandbar out there offers a place to play in the water. And Jace has done a fabulous job of bringing fishermen, water skiers, boaters, and vacationers to his place."

Sid nodded and looked out over the water. His eyes then landed on Grace's and he stared for a few moments. He liked looking at her.

Quinn broke the silence. "So tell me how you two met."

Grace nodded at him so he turned to his buddy. "I was having an attack. Turns out Chiefy here was trained as a support dog. She recognized my symptoms from across the road and pulled Grace over. Chiefy helped me through my attack, Grace did too."

He turned his head and smiled at Grace. Her lips turned up into a beautiful smile. "You actually did what you needed to do to get through it yourself. And, with Chiefy. I just came with her."

Sid squeezed her hand. Her words meant more than she'd ever know.

He turned to Quinn. "She's modest."

Quinn chuckled and Jan came over with his drink. "There you are. Jace said you came out here. Did you want to order something to eat?"

"Yeah." He nodded to Sid. "You two eating?"

"Yeah."

They placed their food order and he sat back to relax. He'd been tense during the exchange, and now his back was cramping up.

"So, I got the Knucklehead started today."

Quinn clapped his hands. "That's fantastic. Nice work. That only took what? A couple of days?"

"Right. That's only a small part of what that old girl needs. But, it felt good to get it started."

"I bet it did."

Sid glanced at Grace. "And, you should see the job Grace is doing at her place. She tiled the bathroom and painted. Now she's painting the cabinets."

Quinn leaned forward, crossing his arms on the table. "Well, now we're talking my language. I enjoy chatting about all things construction. Please tell me what you're doing."

"Aside from the things Sid mentioned, after the cabinets are painted, I'll be redoing the floors. I'm using a rubber laminate floor product so I don't have to worry about tenants getting the floors wet and not cleaning them up. Then, new baseboards, paint, and some decorations and I should be ready to start renting. Then my job starts all over with the second house."

Quinn nodded. "I'll tell you what. I've got a couple of guys I need to keep busy. I hire only veterans and one of them happens to be a whiz with those laminate floors. I don't have work for them for a couple of weeks. I'm happy to loan him out to you."

"That's very nice of you. But I'm on a tight budget and can't afford..."

Quinn held up his hand. "I don't mean to charge you. I do some pro bono work from time to time when I need to keep the guys working but don't have the work myself for them. You'd honestly be doing me a favor."

Grace swallowed and he saw her wrestling with this wonderful gift. He squeezed her hand. "That's a great idea and you'll be finished so much sooner and able to start renting. That's your main goal, isn't it?"

"It is." She took a deep breath. Her eyes looked at

Quinn. "If you're sure. It feels like an awful expensive thing to offer me. I don't know how I could repay you."

Quinn laughed. "As I said, I have to keep them working. Many are recovering from PTSD, or other things and need to stay busy. And, I just don't have anything for them right now. The work on Jace's bungalows is wrapping up soon. The office building we're working on in Orlando is nearly complete, so this is perfect timing."

"Wow. I don't know what..." She smiled and her shoulders dropped slightly. "Thank you so much. I can't tell you how nice that will be for me."

Their food came and they ate and chatted. Grace asked for a paper plate so she could feed Chiefy. She always carried a baggie of dog food with her just in case. Jan, the waitress, brought out the plate and Grace poured Chiefy's food on it. Chiefy ate her food, drank from her bowl, and laid back down again.

The bikers started riding up and down Sunset Beach Road, revving their bikes loudly as they drove past the Sandbar.

Sid looked her way. "Jace will call the police back soon enough."

She frowned and even that was pretty. "They are certainly determined to be disruptive."

"That they are."

She finished her chicken wings and wiped her fingers on the little wet wipe brought to their table with their meals.

The bikers rode by again, and sirens were heard following them. Chiefy let out a low bark and Grace petted her back. "It's okay girl. It's none of our business."

Chiefy's tail wagged then she laid back down.

After their meals Quinn grabbed the bill quickly. "Please let me. I would have eaten alone if not for you two being here. So, I've benefitted much more than you. Plus, Grace is helping me keep a couple of my guys busy this week."

Sid nodded. "I get the next one. Promise."

"Promise." Quinn grinned.

Jan returned and took Quinn's credit card. "What are you thinking these days about Blossom Springs and your future, Sid?"

"To be honest, it feels like I belong here. I like working at the Garage with Coop. I'm only working on the Knucklehead. And a couple small things he needed help with. But, overall, I'm not looking to leave anytime soon."

Quinn leaned forward and clapped his friend on the back. "I'm happy as hell to hear that."

Sid's smile grew as if finally saying it out loud made it permanent. When he glanced her way, she smiled brightly at him and he winked at her.

Quinn's phone rang and he stood to leave. "I hate to eat and run, but I've got to take this. Grace, I'll let Sid know about the guys and when they'll be around."

He pulled his phone to his ear..."KCC."

Sid squeezed her hand on the table. "Let me walk you and Chiefy home. Not sure what's up with the bikers, but let's play it safe."

"Okay."

Sid stood. Chiefy jumped up, tail wagging happily. Grace picked up the paper plate on the ground. Sid held his hand out to her, and her heart thumped.

He was an honest-to-goodness real, kind person. He always held the door, or her chair, or her hand. My gosh, it was the hand-holding that got her the most. She loved that he wanted to hold her hand. Her heart thumped heavily every time he reached out for her hand.

They trudged across the warm sand and Sid stopped in front of his little bungalow. "Do you want to see the inside?"

"I would actually." She looked down, "Will Chiefy be able to come inside?"

"Absolutely."

She bent down and vigorously rubbed Chiefy's fur. She'd been laying in the sand, and she didn't want it all tracked into Sid's house. Chiefy shook and Grace stepped back as sand flew in all directions.

Sid unlocked the door and pushed it open, then stepped back to allow her and Chiefy inside. What she found was a neat, tidy little place. The colors were of teals and oranges, to match the water and sun outside. They entered in the living room. The sofa was a soft teal color, low profile with bright pillows. It opened to the kitchen in the back, which was similar in style to her place. She chuckled, "I wonder if the same builder built my houses. The layout is very similar."

He laughed. "I wondered that too. In a small town it's very likely."

"It's very cute in here. I take it Jace already had this one remodeled."

"I guess he started with the one next door, then a fella named Tony Baluco moved in. He is in a band or something and not around much."

"Okay. Well, he has good taste."

"It works. I do think yours will be very nice when it's finished. You add that feminine touch. I say that with all respect. As you can see, there are few pictures on the walls here. No floral arrangements or incidentals on the shelves. That's a guy's decorating style."

She laughed. He was right of course, but she wouldn't have said it out loud.

The bikers drove by again, but this time they weren't as loud and Sid moved to the back of the house and looked out the back door in the kitchen to see where they went. Grace watched Chiefy sniff all the furniture, the rugs, the door. She was checking the entire place out.

Sid came back and his jaw was set. She felt her shoulders tense up and her back straightened.

"They're sitting outside watching your place."

Her right hand laid over her belly as it quelled slightly. "Okay."

"Stay here." His voice was soft. "I'll get a bowl of water for Chiefy. She's already eaten. I can sleep on the sofa if it makes you more comfortable. But, that way you won't be alone. And I'll be able to sleep because I'll know you aren't in danger."

She swallowed the knot that formed in her throat. "Okay."

She responded quickly because frankly, those guys were getting on her nerves and she didn't want to be alone, though she wouldn't have asked Sid to stay with her.

She inhaled a deep breath and let it out slowly to try and relax her body. It didn't work completely, but it worked a bit.

15

S id sucked in a couple of breaths. He wasn't going to let those assholes break him. They couldn't force him to work on their bikes. Not at all. All they were doing was making him realize there's no way in hell he'd ever work with them. What's the worst they could do? At this point, he didn't care much about himself, but they were focusing on Grace. That was how they thought they'd get to him. And, truth be told, it did make him waver, but he wasn't going to cave in. It was stupid of them to think he'd want to work with them now.

"Okay. Let me get you a t-shirt to sleep in." He took a step toward the bedroom, then stopped. "Wait, I'll get Chiefy water." Maneuvering through the kitchen, he pulled an older bowl from the cupboard and filled it with water. "Does she like ice in it?"

Grace chuckled. "You don't need to add ice. She just plays with the cubes, pulls them out of the water, and scoots them around the floor."

He chuckled.

Setting the bowl on the floor he whistled and Chiefy trotted into the kitchen. "Here you go, girl."

She sniffed the water, looked up at him. "Go ahead." She sniffed again then dipped her tongue in it. It must have been fine, because she lapped at it a couple of times then went into the living room and sat by Grace.

He swooped down the hall to the bedroom and pulled a clean t-shirt from his drawer. He scooted toward the living room then stopped in the bathroom and pulled out the wrapped toothbrush that had been waiting here for him when he arrived. He set it on the counter, then pulled the little tube of toothpaste from the shelf in the medicine cabinet and laid it next to the toothbrush.

When he entered the living room, Grace sat on the sofa, petting Chiefy and speaking softly to her.

He watched them for a moment. His heart swelled when he saw her gentle nature soothing the confused Chiefy.

She turned her head to look into his eyes. "I a..." He cleared his throat. "I have this t-shirt for you to sleep in. There was a toothbrush and toothpaste tube here when I arrived, but I have my own, so I set those out for you in the bathroom. I'm not sure what else you might need."

She smiled. "I'm a bit dusty, would it be alright if I took a shower?"

"Of course." He hurried to the bathroom and dug the shampoo and conditioner left for him out of the top drawer. He sped back into the living room with a huff. "I have pulled the shampoo and conditioner out for you too."

She kissed the top of Chiefy's head, then walked toward him slowly. She stopped a breath away from him. They stood toe to toe. "Thank you."

Her hair was dark but he saw some auburn or red streaks in it as the final rays of sun streamed in through the window. "You're welcome. I'm sorry I'm not better prepared. I haven't had a guest here at all since I've been here, so if you need anything, please ask."

Her lips formed a soft smile. Her eyes were soft as they stared back at him. She was everything he loved in a woman. She was smart, independent, but gentle and sweet. His throat dried as he stared at her. She stood up on her toes and touched her lips to his. It was brief. Far too brief, and he wanted more. But, she backed away a step, then brushed passed him. "I'll be out shortly."

She disappeared into the bathroom. The door closed and he heard the lock click. He grinned, then he heard a motorcycle drive by on the road behind his place and in front of Grace's.

He moved to the kitchen and looked out the window. There was another bike sitting with the first one. He sat in a chair in the kitchen, practicing his deep breathing. Chiefy approached and laid her head on his lap. He instantly put his hand on her head and watched her solemn brown eyes as they stared ahead. She was patiently waiting to see if he needed more or not. He shook his head. "You're something, pretty girl." Her tail swished on the floor a couple of times and he pet her head and back, feeling much better. He'd keep his phone near him tonight, and if anything happened, he'd call the police immediately.

The water in the shower turned on and he stood, patting Chiefy once more. Moving to the refrigerator, he looked inside and noticed he only had a couple of bottles of beer. They'd just eaten so he wasn't hungry, but he could offer popcorn if Grace wanted something.

Moving to the living room his phone rang and he saw Jace's picture on his screen. "Hey, Jace. What's up?"

I just saw the bikers behind your bungalow, looking at Grace's place."

"Yeah. We're aware. Grace is here and staying tonight."

Jace chuckled a bit. "You seem smitten with her."

His stomach twisted around at the thought of being smitten. It had been years. Honestly years.

"I am. It's sudden. Unexpected. But, welcome."

"Good. You deserve someone good in your life. She seems good. I've been asking around about her. The folks I've spoken to have said she's solid."

"Thanks for asking around. I won't say anything."

Jace laughed. "I have to look out for my bud."

"Thanks, Jace."

"Are you going to be alright?"

"It seems like they don't know we're here, they're focusing on her place."

"That's what I was thinking, but you both are welcome to stay at my place. It isn't far and I have security."

"Thank you for the invitation. Grace is taking a shower right now. I'll ask her when she comes out and let you know. I do appreciate the offer."

"Anytime, bud."

The call ended, and the water turned off in the shower. He sat on the sofa and waited for Grace to come out of the bathroom.

O h, the shower felt so good. She'd worked hard today and the dust stuck to the sweat on her skin. She was slightly embarrassed to have met Sid's friends looking as she did. But, things happened kind of fast and her new outlook on life was to go with the flow. So, if they didn't like her because she worked hard, sweated, and got dirty, they just weren't her people.

She squeezed the water from her hair and wrapped a towel around it. With a second towel, she dried off and slipped Sid's t-shirt over her body. It hung nearly to her knees, which was good. She scrunched her face a bit at the thought of putting on her dirty underwear, but she had no choice. It simply was not in her DNA to go without. No matter that she was the new Grace. New Grace, just like old Grace, was not slutty.

She hurried and shimmied them up without thinking too hard about it. Then she brushed her teeth and exited the bathroom. It was cooler in the hall, she must have really steamed up the bathroom. But that hot water felt so darned good. When she entered the living room, Sid sat on the sofa petting Chiefy. Her heart swelled watching them together. She quietly watched them for a few moments to make sure he wasn't dealing with an attack. But, he turned his eyes to hers and his lips creased in the most magnificent smile she'd seen on him. It was nearly breathtaking.

"Hi. Your girl and I are just having a moment of quiet here."

"Thank you for helping her settle in. Tonight will be unusual for her and she's likely a bit out of sorts just now. But, she'll be good. She doesn't have accidents."

He chuckled. "I didn't think she did, and I was not at all worried about her. It's natural for her to feel that something is off. It is. We'll help her through it."

Oh man! He was simply the most fantastic man she'd ever met in her life. Her heartbeat raced and a shiver scooted up her spine.

But, his lips then turned down slightly. "There are now two bikers outside watching your place. Jace called, he's watching too. He said we're welcome to come to his place. I'm fine with whatever you want to do though."

She entered the room and sat on the end of the sofa. Chiefy moved to her for some attention. "I'm okay here as long as they don't find us. But, the issue is, Chiefy will need to go outside before bed. What if they see us?"

Sid nodded slightly but his eyes didn't leave hers. "We can stay close to the house here and make it quick. If they see us and make noise, we can go to Jace's then."

She let out a breath. One more move tonight wasn't something she was interested in. "I had wondered if I should call the police back and at least go inside my place to get some things while they keep the bikers occupied.

Chiefy will need food in the morning and I'll need clothes for tomorrow. Maybe a brush for my hair."

Sid leaned over and slowly pulled the towel off her hair. "Your hair is beautiful." His fingers slid through her wet locks.

Her cheeks heated as did her chest. She swallowed to wet her throat as she stared into his eyes. She knew when she accepted his offer to stay the night it might lead to them actually being together. She liked him so much. It had been so very long since she'd felt feminine and pretty and valuable. It had been years since a man held her interest for more than a minute. She usually walked away as soon as a man spoke to her when she was at a birthday party or wedding of one of her friends back home. She just couldn't go there. Not ever again. Panic welled up inside her so fast she thought she'd actually throw up. But...not with Sid. Maybe because he was damaged too. Maybe because he was vulnerable too.

The back of Sid's fingers brushed her cheek then slid into her hair. "You're beautiful, Grace. Simply beautiful."

Her eyes welled with tears. When was the last time she'd heard that? "Thank you."

She blinked to dry her eyes. She leaned closer to Sid and kissed his lips. His arms wrapped around her and pulled her closer. Her right hand cupped the side of his face, her thumb swept along his cheekbone. His skin was rougher in texture, whiskers and sun did that, but his eyes were sincere and steady when he looked at her. The deep brown was such a pretty color to look at. Their lips met again, this time his tongue licked along her lips. Her tongue met his and they danced together until his tongue swept inside her mouth and slid along her tongue. His lips covered hers. A sizzle erupted up her spine, goose bumps formed on her arms and in her chest, her heartbeat increased. At the same time excitement welled up and created a whole new sensation in her body that she'd never felt before. She felt like an electric current had run through her and her breathing came in spurts.

His hands slid up her ribs, then cupped her breasts. Her nipples pebbled so hard they were sensitive and when his thumb brushed over them, a jolt ran down her tummy to her core. She tensed her muscles, unused to sensations in her nether regions. Her body was so unused to these feelings she worried she'd explode.

His lips softened and felt incredible on hers. They moved and melded with hers perfectly.

She pulled back slightly, a bit embarrassed that he'd see her body in the light of the room. She'd gained a few pounds over the past few years. She'd thought of losing weight or maybe exercising, but honestly, she didn't have the time. She also didn't make healthy meals much of the time, it was just her.

"Can we go to the bedroom?"

His voice was husky and his breath warm as it brushed her cheek. "Of course."

17

S id checked the locks once more, then took Grace's hand and walked side by side to the bedroom. Of course he wanted her. He'd thought about her nearly nonstop since their first meeting. He'd never met a woman like her. Never. Even his ex-wife wasn't on the same level as Grace.

But, yes, now he was nervous. It had been a long time since he'd had a relationship. It had been years. His divorce was ugly and unsettling in so many ways, especially after her attorney had accused him of being unstable. His PTSD had never made him unstable in the way they inferred. He wasn't a danger to anyone. He just had attacks and had to work through them. His ex-wife never understood, or tried to understand what he was going through. She always accused him of being sensitive, as if that made him weak and less of a man. He'd even started to believe her. They'd stopped having sex long before their divorce. He struggled with erections and intimacy. Of course she blamed him for all of it.

Once he found a counselor and started with therapy,

he understood the problem was with her, not him. After the divorce, his attacks came less and less often. And, speaking to his friends, Jace, Quinn, and Myles, he knew he'd get better. They all did it in a different way, but they were all getting healthy.

They entered the bedroom, Chiefy close behind them. He opened his closet door and pulled a blanket out. Laying it on the floor for Chiefy, he patted it and she laid on it nicely. He patted her head, "Good girl."

When he stood, Grace was watching him with a soft smile on her face. He stepped closer to her and pulled her to his body. Their lips met, softly. He felt her shiver and pulled back. "I'm sorry, you're cold."

She shook her head. "I'm not. I'm not cold."

His brows furrowed as he stared into her eyes. Her cheeks turned pink, so did the tips of her ears. He swallowed a dry lump in his throat. "Scared?"

She giggled slightly. "No. Not scared either. I get chills when you touch me. When we're kissing, my body responds. It's puzzling to me too. I've never felt like this with anyone before."

Oh, man, that giant lump grew in his throat. He swallowed a few times to get it to go away and when he was able to speak once more, "Grace..." His fears began to rise up and he wasn't sure he could put his voice to them.

"Sid." She took a deep breath. "I'm nervous too. How about we remove the pressure we're putting on ourselves and just see where this takes us. If we feel it isn't right at any time, we'll stop."

It was his turn to chuckle. "I can handle that."

His lips touched hers once more and her arms slid around his waist. Her body pulled up against his felt so good. The fact she was in his t-shirt was a turn-on. The fact she wasn't wearing a bra right now was sexier. He could feel her nipples pressed to his chest and as his hands roamed down her body, she felt right. Of course, she was feminine and her womanly body against his was exciting in itself. But, she felt right. This felt right. If someone were to ask him what that meant, he couldn't explain it.

He slowly walked her back to the bed, their lips still kissing, touching, teasing each other. Once they reached the bed, he pulled away slightly, leaned forward and pulled the covers back. He tugged his t-shirt from his body and unbuckled his jeans. As he lowered the zipper, he saw Grace pull his t-shirt over her head. She shyly laid on the bed and tucked her feet and legs under the covers. She kept her body slightly hidden from him by crossing her arms over her chest.

Removing his briefs, he slid in next to her and pulled her naked body tightly to his. They laid on their sides, facing each other, their lips still mingling, tasting each other.

His hands found her breasts and enjoyed the fullness in them. Her skin was so soft in his roughened hands, he felt embarrassed. He stopped massaging her breasts and she pulled back slightly. "What?"

"My hands are rough."

She laughed. "I love that about you. You're a man who works with his hands. I find that sexy."

She kissed his lips and his hands went back to exploring her body.

After enjoying her breasts for a while, he slid his hand down the side of her body and over the slope of her hip. He brushed his hand around to the cheeks of her ass, something he'd visually enjoyed for a while now. He squeezed her tightly and pulled her to him tighter. The erection he had bobbed as her body pulled tightly to his. He moved his hips back and forth, enjoying the feel of her skin against his cock.

Grace moved her hands around his body to his ass and tightened her arm to pull him even tighter. Something he'd thought impossible.

His breathing became ragged, his excitement growing to a feverish level. His fingers shook slightly as he explored her body.

Grace pulled his body over hers, spreading her legs to make room for him. He nestled himself between her legs, his cock was hard and feverish, the feel of her soft skin against it was comforting.

He pulled back slightly to stare into the blue irises he looked forward to seeing each day. "I don't have a condom."

She laughed out loud then said, "I never thought of that and never dreamed I'd hear it at my age."

He chuckled. "I know what you mean. I can't believe I'm saying it. But, I want you to know I care for you and want you to feel comfortable. I've not had sex in literally years. As embarrassing as it is to say out loud."

She swallowed and took a deep breath. "Me too. I've been scared."

"Are you scared now?"

She shook her head, her eyes stared deeply into his eyes. "I'm not scared of you, Sid."

His throat dried. This beautiful woman made his emotions go haywire. She was - everything.

He kissed her lips again. Softly. Slowly.

She pushed her body against his, making his cock pulse.

He lifted his body slightly, positioned the head of his cock at her entrance and whispered, "Are you sure?"

"Yes." Her response came instantly.

He slowly pushed himself into her body. The feeling he had before of her soft skin against his cock was nothing like the warmth as her body wrapped him completely. He thought he'd lose his breath and his body shook as an electric jolt raced through him.

He moved slowly at first, enjoying how her body accepted him time after time. Her soft body under him felt incredible. Her arms wrapped around his torso and held tightly as her knees rose into the air, allowing him more access to her softness.

His brain was trying to catch up with all of his feelings.

He pushed in further and she moaned. She whispered something but he couldn't hear it. Pulling out, he pushed back in faster. His balls began to tighten, his body shook. That delectable pain associated with pleasure started at the base of his cock. He moved faster in her. "Grace. I want you to come first."

She moaned softly and her arms tightened around him. He dropped his head near her ear and whispered, "Baby, come for me."

Her body stiffened and her arms squeezed him tightly. His excitement rose and he pushed in again. His balls drew up painfully into his body and his release poured from him, that searing glorious pain that they'd worked toward.

Grace woke to the sound of glass breaking. Chiefy barked and ran to the bedroom door. Finding it closed, she ran to Grace who reached out and petted her. "It's okay, girl."

She hoped it was anyway. Breaking glass sounded again. Her heartbeat sped up and her throat dried. The bed moved as Sid stood and pulled on his underwear. He dug through a drawer in his dresser and pulled a pair of sweatpants from inside. He slipped those on. His voice was gravelly when he said, "Stay in here."

He quickly stepped from the room and closed the door behind him. Grace sat up, but listened, Chiefy ran to the door. A loud sound like something hitting something hard, then glass shattered again. Chiefy barked.

Grace hurried to pull on her panties and Sid's t-shirt. She got brave and rummaged in the drawer she saw him pull his sweatpants from and found a pair of sweatpants for herself. She shimmied them on, then waited with Chiefy for Sid.

The door opened and he stepped inside. "Nothing

here is broken, but as I looked out the kitchen window, I heard another window break at your place. I heard them laughing. Then they heard Chiefy barking and began looking over here. You call the police, I'll call Jace."

Grace fumbled for her phone and dialed 911.

"911 what's your emergency?"

"Hi, my name is Grace Murphy and I live at forty-two Sunset Beach Road. Someone just threw something through my windows."

"Okay, I'm sending officers over there now. Are you safe?"

"Yes, I was staying across the street with a friend." Her cheeks burned. She felt like a teenager sharing for the first time she'd slept with a man. But, good grief, she was fifty years old. And they were consenting adults. She simply didn't share details like that with anyone. Not that she did just now either.

"Okay. Stay there, police are on their way."

"Thank you."

The call ended as Sid finished tying his shoes. He pulled his phone off the bedside table and dialed up Jace.

Sid put his call on speaker so she could hear it. Jace's voice sounded wide awake. "Hey, what's up?"

"I think the bikers broke windows at Grace's and heard Chiefy barking here. I'm afraid they're focusing on this place now."

"Come on over. I'm on Classified Drive. I think you've been cutting across my driveway to and from the Garage."

"Are you shittin' me?"

Jace laughed. "No. I don't tell a lot of people where I live. Quinn only knows because he's the only one I trust to do work for me. So, there's that."

"How do you know I've been cutting across?"

Jace chuckled. "I have security cameras."

"Shit. Well, I'm sorry if I shouldn't have been crossing there."

"Bud, if I cared, I'd have said something. Come on over."

"We'll be there after the police leave."

"I'll be ready."

Sirens began breaking the silence of the area and Chiefy started barking again.

He tapped the end-call icon and looked at Grace. He grinned when he saw her in his sweatpants. "Glad you found something to wear."

"Thank goodness you had something with a draw-string." She held up his t-shirt to show him how much of the string hung down.

"Okay. We'll get in my truck and drive over. I don't know what those assholes are willing to do and I don't want to take chances. We'll head to Jace's after the police leave. We'll figure out tomorrow - tomorrow."

"Okay." She scrapped her hands through her hair and took a deep breath. Never in a million years would she have thought she'd be in a situation like this. "Can I grab some things from my place too?"

"Of course. I'll help you gather up some things for Chiefy while you pack your things."

He opened the bedroom door and Chiefy ran out, still barking. As Grace started through the door he dropped his arm to stop her. Turning her head to look at him, he grinned. "I need a kiss first."

She chuckled, then rose up on her toes and kissed his lips. Not a hardship at all and she liked that he'd taken the time to ask for a kiss when they needed to meet the police.

She stepped into the hallway then stopped short.

Would this cause him to have an attack? She'd watch carefully, and Chiefy would be with them too, so she'd certainly take care of Sid.

Sid bumped into her from behind. "What's up, Grace?"

She shook her head quickly. "Nothing. A thought ran through my head, and it caused me to stop. It's all good."

Sid's strong hands on her shoulders turned her around. They stood toe to toe. She tipped her head back to look up at him.

His voice was calm. "I'm okay. I know you've seen me have a PTSD attack, and one close call, but I'm fine."

She swallowed. "Do you feel them coming on?"

"Sometimes. Not the day of the fireworks though. Those caught me off-guard. That's why it happened."

"Okay."

She took a deep breath, kissed him quickly as sirens drew closer, then turned and found her shoes in the living room. She tied them as Sid put Chiefy's leash on her collar.

He nodded to her, "Ready?"

"Yeah."

He opened the door and Chiefy ran out first. Grace chuckled as Sid was taken off-guard at her strength. Chiefy stopped to pee and Sid unlocked his truck with the key fob.

Her fingers shook slightly as she climbed into Sid's truck. Soon, he opened the back door and Chiefy jumped inside and gave Grace's cheek a big sloppy lick. Chiefy loved car rides.

Sid jumped in and started his truck. He backed out of the driveway and swung the truck toward Grace's. They were basically across the street from each other, but he was right, she felt better in the truck rather than standing outside and being vulnerable to those bikers.

The police cars had already parked in her driveway, and she got out of the truck and waited for the officers, who had flashlights and were walking around her place, to approach her.

"Ma'am, is this your house?"

"Yes. I'm Grace Murphy. I called 911."

"My name is Officer Isak Voss."

"Hello, Officer Voss."

"It does appear there are two windows broken. Do you have any idea who did this?"

"Yes. I'm reasonably sure it was that biker gang who've been hanging around town the past week or so."

"Why do you feel it's them?"

"Because they've been sitting here on the road, watching my place, which is why I stayed with my friend."

Sid approached from the driver's side of the truck. She smiled at him, though it was dark and he likely couldn't see her. "This is my friend, Sid Hoffman. Sid, this is Officer Voss."

"Mr. Hoffman, I'll ask you some questions in a moment."

Sid nodded but stood by.

Another officer approached them. Officer Voss turned briefly, then introduced them. "Officer Erin Moody, this is Grace Murphy, owner of the home and Sid Hoffman, her friend."

Officer Moody nodded. "I found bricks laying inside on the floor in the glass. Do you mind opening the door and letting us inside?"

"No." Her fingers shook as she pulled her keys from her little shoulder bag. Never in her life, that she could remember, and she'd have remembered this, did she have to let police officers in her home.

Sid stepped closer and held his hand out. "I can do it, Grace."

Tears sprang to her eyes instantly. She sniffed, but nodded and handed Sid her keys. Then she took in a deep cleansing breath. She'd done nothing wrong.

Officer Voss moved with Sid to the house and Officer Moody stayed with her. Her voice was soft, but confident when she asked, "Have you had issues with this biker gang before today?"

She swallowed, "Only since two days ago. They bothered Sid..." She pointed to the house. "At the Garage two days ago. I stopped in right after, and they had a biker sitting on his bike, watching the Garage and saw me and Sid chatting. One of them followed me home. He sat outside on his motorcycle all day. I'm remodeling. Anyway, they watched my house all day."

"Why do you think they did that?"

"They want Sid to be their main mechanic. He said no. They're trying to scare us. Him. Scare him into saying yes. He doesn't want to work with them. Last night we went to the Sandbar to eat dinner and they were there. They started trouble and Jace...he's the owner...called the police and the bikers were asked to leave. It made them mad. They drove back and forth up and down the street for a while until the police...you guys...girls...officers made them stop."

Grace swallowed. "I'm sorry. I'm nervous."

Officer Moody chuckled slightly. "There's nothing for you to be nervous about."

Grace shrugged, "Except the bikers are beginning to escalate their actions."

"Right. Except that."

Grace turned to the officer. She was pretty. Her hair was pulled back, but her skin was clear and her eyes were a pretty light blue. She looked to be a little bit younger than Grace. Though Grace was terrible at guessing ages.

"Isn't there anything we can do to protect ourselves against these guys?"

Officer Moody turned to face her. Her lips turned down into a frown. "I'm afraid there isn't much we can do to help you. If you feel threatened and they are watching your place, we can ask them to move on. But until they do something, like this, we have to operate under the law and that is they haven't done anything until they have."

"But they've been a nuisance in town for a while now."

"Yes. But they're smart and they know how far they can push things to not get in too much trouble."

19

I t took more than an hour, but they each spoke to officers and told them what happened. The officers now waited in their squad car for Grace to pack up a few things and them to leave for Jace's.

Sid watched Grace's face as she glanced around at the mess. "Don't think about it tonight. Walk around the glass. We'll come back tomorrow and sweep it up and cover the windows until we can get them fixed."

"But, there will be bugs in here tomorrow."

He nodded. "Right. How about this? Do you have plastic wrap? Get me that and some tape. I'll cover the windows so bugs can't get in. It won't be great, but it'll do better than nothing. Then we'll head over to Jace's."

"Okay." Grace stepped carefully around the glass on the floor. Sid noticed a broom propped in the corner and swept some of the glass away from the windows into small piles. Grace came back with plastic wrap and tape and he worked on closing up the windows that had been broken while Grace packed.

He finished as she came out of the bedroom with a

backpack, filled to bursting. He chuckled. "We're only staying one night."

She shrugged. "But, I didn't plan on staying at your place last night and I'm not sure what will happen tonight, so I'm trying to be prepared. Plus, I thought a suitcase was a bit much."

He laughed and moved closer to her. He bent and kissed her lips. "You're awesome."

"Because I can pack?"

"Because you make me happy."

She cocked her head to the right and a small smile lifted her lips. "You make me happy too."

His heart pounded in his chest. He hadn't heard those words in so long from someone else. He'd never thought about it all these years, but hearing them now made him realize how important it was to hear someone you cared about say them.

"Thank you," he whispered. He kissed the top of her head and sucked in a deep breath.

Grace glanced at the windows. "Thank you for closing up the windows. I appreciate it."

"You're welcome. Let's try to get some sleep now."

"Okay." She stepped toward the door, then stopped. "I have to get Chiefy's food."

Grace hurried into the kitchen and Sid bent and picked up Chiefy's bowls and rinsed them out. He looked around, "Does she have toys?"

Grace laughed. "Any stick outside, anything she pulls from the water, and occasionally I buy her pig ears."

"Okay. Do you have any pig ears here for her? It might make her more comfortable."

"You're sweet on Chiefy," she chided. Opening a cupboard, she pulled out a bag that held one lone pig ear.

He chuckled and picked up Chiefy's food and dishes. They walked side by side to the front door. Outside, Chiefy patiently waited for them in the truck, and he chuckled when he saw his windows.

"She's been panting a lot in there, my windows are all steamed up."

Grace laughed. "She does that."

He opened the back door and set her food and dishes on the floor. Chiefy began sniffing wildly, her tail smacking the back of the seats.

Grace opened the passenger back door and set her backpack on the floor on the other side. Chiefy turned and licked Grace's cheek a couple of times. Grace giggled and petted her pup, and he couldn't stop watching them. Watching them together was a joy.

He walked around the truck quickly and opened the passenger door for Grace. She smiled and looked into his eyes and he made the mental note to do that all the time so he would be the recipient of one of her smiles.

He waited for her to step up into his truck, then closed the door. As he walked around behind the truck, he waved at the police officers watching over them.

He pulled from her driveway and turned the truck right on Sunset Beach Road. Then he turned right on Main Street. Looking at the Garage as he drove past, he noted all looked well, which he was both grateful for and thought was weird. Why focus on Grace? Except, she was likely considered his Achilles heel. And that wasn't far from the truth. He was growing incredibly fond of her. He looked forward to spending time with her.

He swallowed the lump that grew in his throat and turned right onto Classified Drive. He should have known something was up with Classified Drive. All the other streets here had simple names. First Street. The alley between Main Street and Classified Drive was named Alley. Nothing here was overly complicated, which was one of the things he enjoyed so much about this town.

He turned right again as Classified Drive swept to the right and there it was. A huge house at the end of the street. He'd never looked before because it was largely concealed by palm trees. But, now that he'd driven past those, the large white house stood out as a masterpiece on a canvas.

Grace sat forward. "Holy cow."

"That's what I was thinking."

"You didn't know he had this huge house?"

"Nope."

He stopped at the base of the steps leading up to the front doors. Massive double doors painted white to match the house were adorned with brass knockers.

He swallowed, not sure he knew what to think with this revelation. He'd always known Jace to be down-to-earth and carefree. This place must take an enormous amount of effort to keep up.

Shutting the truck off, he jumped down and walked around the front of the truck to open Grace's door. As soon as she stepped down, she turned to stare once more at the house, then moved to let Chiefy out.

He opened Chiefy's door for her, Grace grabbed Chiefy's leash, and as soon as Chiefy jumped down, she sniffed around looking for a place to pee.

Sid shook his head and chuckled. This didn't look like a place that anyone would pee, but then again, Chiefy was really quite special, and a dog.

One of the front doors opened and Jace stepped out. He held his arms wide. "Welcome, friends. Welcome."

Chiefy barked and Grace bent to pet her and soothe her. "It's okay, girl."

Sid pulled Grace's backpack out of the truck along with Chiefy's food. The three of them walked up to Jace, both in awe and grateful for a place this nice to sleep in.

Jace laughed. "Welcome to my place."

Jace stepped aside and waited for them to walk in, then he stepped in and closed the door.

"This is incredible, Jace."

"Thank you. This used to be the home of a former governor, who lived here before he went to Tallahassee to govern. He was wealthy and he had grand taste. He never came back to live here after he stopped governing. Instead, he moved out of state, to places unknown. There was a bit of a scandal here before he left that he was having an affair with one of the daughters of one of his big-time donors. So, he was afraid to come back. At least, that's the rumor people love to tell. But, it sat empty for a number of years by the time I got here. It needed a ton of work, but I liked the location and the story behind it, so I bought it. To this day the townspeople call it the Governor's Mansion."

20

G race patted Chiefy. "Sit."

Chiefy sat and Jace chuckled. "She's good here. You can let her off the leash."

"Are you sure?"

"I'm sure. Come on in and make yourselves comfortable."

Grace looked up at Sid and he nodded.

She unhooked Chiefy's leash and she started sniffing the floors, rugs, furniture, everything. Grace chuckled, "That will help her sleep."

Jace nodded. "Good. I'm just about ready for bed, so let me show you your room."

Grace shrugged. "I'm sorry it's so late."

Jace chuckled. "It's not late for me. The bar closed at two, then I do some cleanup to take the edge off. I'd just gotten home when Sid called."

There was a large, curved staircase that swept along the wall to the right. Jace started up the staircase. Sid waited for her to follow him, then he followed behind her. Chiefy was close behind.

At the top of the staircase Grace glanced down below and the view was stunning. She could see into the living room which was beautifully decorated. It was masculine and comfortable, but also very appealing.

Jace chuckled. "I hired a designer when I bought this place. It had been empty for some time and wasn't in the greatest condition. I hired Quinn to do all the construction work. The designer worked with Quinn to get everything looking as it does. I hire a cleaning lady once a week to come in and clean everything and a gardener to keep the grounds mowed and the landscaping cleaned up. I don't want snakes or anything slithery living in there."

"I don't blame you," she said.

Jace turned right at the top of the stairs and opened a door. "This is your room. You're all welcome here as long as you want to stay. I'm not here much. I have weird sleeping patterns since my time in the military and don't sleep more than four or five hours at a clip."

Sid nodded. "I get that. And we thank you."

"How bad was the damage?"

Sid looked into her eyes a moment, then at Jace. "Two broken windows. They used bricks, not sure where they found them. But they hurled them through the windows. I happened to be looking outside when the second one happened, but I didn't actually see them throw it. I heard them laughing, then they heard Chiefy barking and stopped to look at my place. I hope they don't try something there."

"I have security by the bar, but not the bungalows. But that will change tomorrow. Those guys have been ripping up the town. I've finally found a nice little place I enjoy, and those assholes are trying to take over."

Grace nodded. "The police officer I spoke with told me

their hands are tied. They can't really do anything about them unless they actually do something illegal or, like you did last night, a citizen calls to complain. Then they can ask them to leave. But, until those things happen, they can't do anything else."

Sid shook his head. "That's bullshit."

Jace nodded. "I agree. If they keep scaring people, tourism will fall off and that's my bread and butter."

Grace frowned. "That's mine too. I hope they don't scare people away and how will I protect myself legally if they harm any of my tenants?"

Jace looked straight at her. "That might be something that has to be asked of the city council."

Now that was a good idea. Maybe she'd look into something like that. Find out when the next meeting is and go to it.

Jace stepped into the hall. "Make yourselves at home. If Chiefy needs to go outside, at the bottom of the steps make a left and the kitchen is around the corner. There's a door that leads to a small backyard. There's food in the fridge if you get hungry. I'm a hands-off host, so you'll need to get comfortable fast."

He chuckled and closed the door behind him.

Sid set her backpack on the bed and looked around the room. There was an attached bathroom to the left of the bed. He filled Chiefy's water bowl and set it on the tiled bathroom floor.

Chiefy began lapping at the water and Sid chuckled. "Which side of the bed do you want?" He asked.

She grinned and shrugged. "I guess it doesn't matter to me. I prefer the right side, but I will sleep just fine on the left. You pick."

He wrapped his arms around her and kissed the top of

her head. "It doesn't matter to me either. But I sure am tired."

"Me too."

He stepped away and turned the light off. She picked up her backpack and carried it into the bathroom. She found her pajamas, which were little shorts and a tank top. But, she'd feel better with them on and a clean pair of underwear.

She quickly changed her clothes, brushed her teeth and ran a brush through her hair. It was a mess of snarls and she shook her head thinking that Jace must have thought she was quite the wreck. He was probably texting Sid right now asking him what on earth he was thinking.

She turned the bathroom light off and opened the door. Sid had a bedside lamp on for her. Chiefy laid on a blanket on the floor near the door, her preferred spot. She smiled at her pup and Sid's thoughtfulness and slid into bed.

Sid scooted to the middle and pulled her into his arms from behind. He nestled his nose in the crook of her neck and hummed in appreciation. "You smell good."

She sighed. Life was unpredictable on the best of days. Never in her wildest dreams would she have thought she'd meet a great man in such a short time after moving here. Actually, at all. Never would she have thought of ever meeting someone like Sid.

She let her body relax. It had been a long day. Filled with many firsts. Free help thanks to Quinn Kurtz. Her house vandalized. And, she and Sid had sex for the first time. Her eyes closed as her heart felt happy.

21

S id heard someone moving around downstairs and Chiefy let out a low bark. Grace sat upright and looked around the room. Chiefy ran to her and got some morning hugs and kisses.

Grace turned to him and smiled. "Good morning."

"Good morning. You look beautiful."

She laughed. "I doubt that, but it sure feels good to hear it."

He sat up and pulled her close. His lips met hers and Chiefy whined. Grace chuckled and he pulled back, reluctantly.

"You get dressed. I'll take Chiefy outside."

"Thank you. I can do it if you'd like to rest a while longer."

He stared into her eyes, still happy to look into them and still so enamored with the color. "No. I'll go down and talk to Jace for a bit. Do you like coffee in the morning?"

"Yes. I do. Just cream, no sugar."

"You got it." He pulled back the covers and reached for his clothes as the bathroom door closed.

Pulling on his sweatpants and t-shirt from last night, he chuckled as Chiefy pranced around. "Come on pretty girl, let's get you outside."

Chiefy jumped up and her tail thumped as she followed him down the stairs. He turned left as Jace directed last night and found the kitchen at the back of the house.

Jace sat at the kitchen table in front of a window, a cup of coffee in front of him, and the paper opened on the table.

"Good morning. I hope I didn't wake you."

Sid chuckled. "No. We want to get an early start of it today. And Chiefy needs to go out. We'll be right back in."

He opened the back door which led into a sunroom. Or actually a Florida room, because it had actual windows in it.

Opening the door that led outside, Chiefy bounded out to the back yard and ran around, sniffing at everything. He looked at the beautiful landscaping and area. You'd never know this house was basically in the middle of town. The way it was situated on a cul-de-sac and surrounded by palm trees, it looked like a dense woods from the outside. He chuckled. Leave it to Jace to find this little gem in town.

Chiefy finally peed but continued to sniff. He wanted a cup of coffee and to chat with Jace, but he let Chiefy have some fun before calling her inside.

Finally, Chiefy looked up to see if he was still there and that's when he patted his leg. "Come on, girl. Let's go in."

She ran to him and he thought once more what a great dog she was. So well- behaved.

As they entered the house once more, Jace stood at the coffee pot refilling his cup. "You want one?"

"Yes. Please. Grace will be down in a minute too."

"Two coffees coming up. I'll pour, but you'll have to doctor it on your own."

Sid chuckled. "Deal."

Jace poured and Sid sat at the table to stay out of the way. Jace moved from the coffee pot, leaving the two poured coffees on the counter and Sid stood and poured cream in one, and left his black.

"Thanks for letting us stay here last night. We appreciate it."

"I meant it when I said it's no problem. I have this big place to myself and it's nice knowing there are others in the house besides my old bones rattling around in here."

"I get it."

Jace closed the newspaper and looked across the table at his friend. "So, what's the future plan?"

Sid shrugged and sipped his coffee. "Immediate future is to make sure these guys don't harm Grace or Chiefy." He glanced at Chiefy who was sniffing the rugs in the kitchen. "I'm not sure how to do that. But, I'm going to do what I can."

"Okay. What about after that?"

Sid chuckled. "You mean am I staying here in Blossom Springs?"

"Yeah."

He looked his friend in the eye. "I'd like to. I'm calmer here - bikers aside. It's a nice little town. I don't have anyone back home. I like the Garage, and if I wanted to, I'm sure Coop would hire me."

Jace nodded. "Here you have Quinn and me."

"Yep." He sipped his coffee again. "I wouldn't move here for you two old farts though."

Jace laughed. "Can't say I blame you."

Grace entered the kitchen looking fresh and beautiful as usual. Chiefy ran to her and she petted her pup, and gave her a kiss on the top of the head. "Good morning." She pointed to the cup of coffee on the counter and Sid nodded.

His attention was on Grace as she carried her coffee to the table. She'd pulled her hair back into a ponytail. She wore a clean pair of jeans and a clean t-shirt. She had tennis shoes on her feet and if he didn't know she was fifty he would easily have said forty. He pulled the chair out next to him and she sat down. She sipped her coffee and Sid watched her. He enjoyed watching her.

Jace chuckled and Sid turned to look at his friend, who had been watching him. Not much got by Jace.

"Jace, how is the bar doing? I mean, you have this magnificent house, but is the bar responsible or was this from money you had saved?"

"A little of both. The bar is going well. I sold my little bar in Missouri before I came down here. I had cash, and nothing to do, as it was. My plan wasn't to buy a bar, but to kick around for a while and figure out what I wanted to do with my life. My divorce was a killer."

Sid nodded. "I remember."

"But, as it turned out, the old man who owned the bar wanted to sell it and I found I sort of liked it here. As I keep renovating and expanding, the bar continues to grow, which is great. We're adding food choices all the time and the patrons are telling us they love what we're doing. Plus, the location is everything and then some. I just have to keep the place from getting run down, and that the location pulls people to it. Plus, I've met some musicians here. They work out of the barn at the end of Sunset Beach Road. Tony, the manager, lives in the bungalow next to you for the time being. I guess he's building a house of his own now, so he won't be there long. And the lead singer, Jami Hart, lives in the farmhouse in front of the barn. They have been coming down here when they're in town and playing gigs on the beach. That's becoming something I need to get more serious about. Having regular music."

Grace smiled sweetly. "I think live music on the beach would be wonderful."

Jace nodded. "I agree. So, before I begin to offer that on a regular basis, I need to make sure I can book the bands I want regularly. That's the next step I think, in the evolution of Sarge's Sandbar."

Grace laughed. "Why do you call it Sarge's?"

Jace shrugged and Sid chuckled. "We had a friend in the service who just couldn't seem to make it past the rank of sergeant. After he was passed up for a few promotions it became a joke. Then, he decided he liked being called Sarge, so that's what we all called him. He died two years ago and it sort of broke my heart a bit. I liked him. So, Sarge's Sandbar it is. Plus, most people don't know I'm not Sarge and that gives me a bit of anonymity."

Sid nodded and Grace turned to him. "Did you know Sarge too?"

He chuckled. "I did. He was a likable guy, but he was not ambitious in the least. Which is why he never rose in rank. He knew that too."

22

Listening to Sid and Jace chat about old times felt nice. Grace went upstairs and brought Chiefy's dishes down. Filling her food bowl and adding fresh water to her water bowl, she smiled as she watched her pup happily eat. She'd managed all this turmoil so well last night and she slept good.

For that matter, Grace slept good last night too. Sid made her feel safe and wanted. It had been years since she'd felt either of those things. It was weird how a person could miss something so much but not realize what it was they were missing.

Jace stood up. "I'm trying a new recipe today. You two can be my guinea pigs."

Grace laughed. "Oh, dear. Well, is there something I can do to help you?"

"Nope. I'm a solitary chef. You and Sid sit there and talk to me."

Sid put his arm around her shoulders and kissed her temple. "He doesn't like anyone hovering about while he's cooking. But, I can tell you he's a great chef. All those recipes on the menu at the Sandbar are Jace's."

"Really?" Jace bowed and they both laughed at him.

Chiefy paced by the door so Grace walked her outside. She enjoyed the warmth of the sun as it rose. Today was supposed to be in the eighties here. She looked forward to that. One of the reasons she chose to move to Florida was for the weather. She could work all day in the sweltering heat and sweat like a pig and it didn't bother her. She just kept herself hydrated. But, she hated the cold.

Some birds began chirping loudly to each other, likely warning that she was out here and Chiefy too. Chiefy squatted and peed, then kept herself busy smelling all the shrubs and bushes in the landscaping. She scared a bird from a bush and ran across the yard as if she'd catch it. She found a frog near the base of a bush and barked at it. Grace laughed at her playfulness. She was nearly five years old and she still acted like a puppy. It was cute.

"Come on, girl. Let's go in."

Chiefy ran to her and she held the door open to let her inside. She immediately ran to her water dish and took a good healthy drink. Grace sat next to Sid at the table and he took her hand in his.

"Your hand is warm."

"It's getting hot out. It's supposed to be in the eighties today."

Jace clapped his hands. "That's excellent news for a bar owner on the beach!"

Grace laughed. Sid's phone rang.

He answered it and stepped away. Grace tried not listening. If he wanted her to know he'd tell her about it. The aroma from the stove wafted over to her at the table. "It smells fantastic, Jace. What are you making?"

"Chorizo steak, hash browns, and eggs. Obviously I've made the hash browns and eggs before, but this chorizo recipe is one I just worked out. So, you and Sid are my taste testers."

"Well, if it tastes anything like it smells, it'll be amazing."

Sid sat at the table. "That was Quinn. He's sending two guys over today and they'll fix your windows."

"Really? That's wonderful."

Sid chuckled and took her hand in his. He stared into her eyes and she stared right back into his. Those deep brown orbs were incredible. Such a beautiful tone of brown and one that spoke to her.

"You two need to stop making googly eyes at each other."

Grace felt her cheeks heat up and Sid laughed. "I don't think you know what that actually means."

"I know what it means. You two stare at each other all the time."

"We do not."

Sid shrugged but he turned to her and winked. He was going to bust Jace's balls a bit.

Jace brought them each a plate of food. The wonderful aromas rising up to meet her were incredible. "Eat while it's hot and I want only honest opinions. Otherwise you can pack up and leave."

She laughed as she picked up her fork. Sid grumbled something but said no more.

The first bite she took was incredible. The steak was absolute perfection, but she didn't want to say that right away, it looked like she was only saying it because they stayed there last night. She took another healthy bite to make sure she really liked it.

She nodded her head and Jace's brows rose into his dark hair. "Yes, it's fantastic."

"Honesty only."

"It's great. I love the blend of spices. I've had chorizo meat before and it was delicious, but this is a bit better. The heat is softer. It comes a bit later, which is a nice surprise. It's also not so hot that my eyes water and it doesn't drown out the flavor of the meat itself."

Jace stopped at the table and stared at her for a long time. She began to fidget then he said, "Do tell how you know all that."

Laying her fork on her plate, she inhaled and swallowed. "I used to manage a seafood restaurant back home in Maine."

Sid leaned back and stared at her, surprise on his handsome face. Jace clapped his hands and laughed. "Now that's fantastic. You'll always be my new taste tester. I promise I'll keep you both fed as long as you give me honest advice."

"Deal."

Sid chuckled. "It's hard to pass up great free food."

She swallowed another bite of her food then asked Sid. "What time is Quinn sending the guys over?"

"He said in an hour."

She looked at her watch. It was six-thirty. She'd slept all of three hours. At the moment she felt wide awake, but the day may sap all her energy later. And, what happened if the bikers came back? She'd make sure to have her phone handy at all times so she could call.

Sid leaned over and softly said, "If you need me to stay at the house, I will. If not, please call me if those bikers come around. I'll be right there and you'll have Quinn's men, one of which is his son, Jared. He's honorable just like his dad."

"He has a son old enough to work for him?"

"He does."

"I thought he only hired former military."

"He does. So, Jared had to go into the service to get a job with his dad." Sid and Jace both laughed.

Jace sat at the table with a plate in front of him. "That's the truth. Quinn said he wasn't breaking that rule for anyone, including his son. Man was his ex-wife spittin' mad. I thought she was going to kill him."

Sid chuckled. "I did too. I offered my place in Minnesota for him to hide in until she calmed down."

Jace grinned. "He wanted to be right here under her nose, so every time she saw him she knew Jared listened to him."

Grace finished her last bite, then said. "I'm glad he came back okay."

Both men stopped and stared at her for a moment. "As a parent, that's a tough call, right? Send him into the military which will make him a man and teach him so much. But, it can also harm him or kill him."

Jace shrugged his shoulders. "It's an honor to serve our country. It's an honor to die for it too. Not that we want to, but it is an honor."

Grace swallowed. It was the truth and one she'd repeated to others in the past.

Sid stood and picked up both their plates. "Are you ready to go, Grace?"

"I am. Let me run upstairs and get my backpack."

Jace nodded. "You can stay tonight again if you need too. The place is here."

She smiled at Jace. He was handsome with his dark hair and olive skin. His eyes were dark brown. But, he was chiseled in a way that he could look hard if he didn't smile. She wondered what his story was, but didn't have time to get into it. "Thank you so much, Jace. I sure do appreciate it."

He waved her away with his fork. "Anytime. Really."

She turned and saw Sid waiting for her in the doorway. "Thanks, bud. I'll talk to you later."

"Keep me up-to-date on the happenings."

23

S id pulled up to Grace's little house and she heaved out a deep breath. "I need to go in and sweep. Can you keep Chiefy out here until I have the glass picked up?"

He chuckled. "Honey, I'll go in with you. Chiefy is fine out here for a few minutes. We'll get the glass picked up and then I'll head over to my place and make sure everything is fine."

She turned her head slowly and looked into his eyes. "I'm so sorry. I didn't even think of that this morning. I apologize I've been so focused on myself and my house."

He reached over and ran the backs of his fingers across her cheek. "Honey, it's fine. You've been dealing with a lot and I'm the one who's sorry for all of this. If it wasn't for the bikers seeing you at the Garage with me, they wouldn't be focused on you."

"You couldn't have known what they'd do."

"No. That's a fact. But, I'm sorry just the same."

Her eyes grew glassy and she blinked. "Thank you."

He slightly shook her shoulder. "That bastard never apologized to you either?"

She chuckled once, then shook her head. "No." She sniffed lightly. "I don't know why I get emotional when you treat me so nicely. It's just all these emotions keep barraging me and making me realize how much I've missed in life. How much I've wanted someone..." She looked into his eyes. "Like you."

It was his turn to have a catch in his throat. His breathing became choppy. "I've missed so much in my life too and I didn't know that until I met you."

Silence fell around them as they looked into each other's eyes. Except for Chiefy's heavy breathing. Then she moved forward and licked Sid on the cheek. He laughed. So did Grace and their serious moment was once again broken by the pup.

He opened his door and hustled around the front of the truck to open Grace's door. The instant he opened it, her smile warmed him like standing in the sun did. She was incredible.

Reaching in, he waited for her to take his hand and help her down. He noticed her cheeks were an adorable shade of pink, and she smelled like citrus.

She pulled her keys from the little shoulder bag she carried and stepped up onto the porch. She stopped cold in front of him and he chuckled. "We've got to stop doing this."

She pointed to the porch floor. "Boot prints. Do you think the police would be able to get a good print from those?"

Sid bent to get a better view, then stood and gently pulled Grace back to him. "I don't know that they'll get a good print, but the concern here is the boot print is wet.

From the wet grass. That had to have happened recently. So, let's go get in the truck and not disturb anything."

"Okay." Her voice shook and he was sorry for it. But, what if someone was lying in wait here?

Grace started back to the truck then stopped. "Aren't you coming too?"

"I'm going to check around the back of the house first."

"It could be dangerous."

"Honey, please get in the truck. I'm only stepping around the side of the house to make sure no one is waiting around for you to come back alone. If you hear anything terrible, call the police."

"But..."

"Babe..."

She nodded. "Okay."

He waited for her to open the door of the truck and climb in. Then, he moved stealthily around the side of the house, between Grace's two bungalows. He watched the ground for footprints or pressed grass. It seemed clear.

He heard rustling and looked up to see the back of one of the bikers running along the footpath he'd taken to get to Main Street. He pulled his phone up and called Jace.

"Yeah."

"One of the bikers is running across your driveway right about now."

He heard rustling then a huff. "Yep. I've got him on camera. I'll pull it down for the police. Did he do anything at Grace's or your place?"

"Not that I've found. We saw a footprint on the deck which is what alerted me to the fact someone was here."

"Okay. Let me know if you find signs of entry or damage."

"Will do."

He hung up and continued to search around the house. Birds flew from their hiding spots in shrubs. He was as startled as they were. He swallowed and continued around the house. When he came back to the truck, Grace let out a long breath. He grinned.

"Everything okay?"

"Yes. I did chase one of the bikers away from the house. He ran down the footpath and Jace saw him on camera. He'll forward that footage to the police. We may be able to get police to watch your place closer now. But, I didn't find any damage to the house."

"Okay." Grace opened the door to get out and he held his hand out to assist her. Not that she needed it, but he wanted to touch her. He wanted to help her, too. He liked being around her.

He closed the truck door and they walked together to the house. Grace dropped her keys and he bent to pick them up. He saw her fingers shaking. "Are you scared?"

She smiled but it didn't reach her eyes. "I ..." She nodded. "Yeah. I guess hearing they were right here on my property scares me. It's one thing to toss a brick or two, that sucks. But, he came right up here on my property."

Sid found the key on her keyring, there were only three and one looked like a padlock key. The other was for the trunk of her car, which left her house key. He unlocked the door and handed her keys back. "Do you want me to go in first?"

"No. We can go in together."

He stepped in first to make sure there weren't any surprises in store for them, then held the door for Grace. She stepped through the door and her jaw was tight. "I'll stay here with you until Quinn's guys get here."

"Really. If you need to get to the Garage I'm sure we'll

be fine. I'll lock the doors and call the police if something happens."

"Grace. I don't work at the Garage, remember? I'm just fixing the old Knucklehead and I help Coop out if he needs it. I can come and go as I like."

She chuckled. "I guess it feels like you work there, and I forgot about you just being there."

He kissed her lips quickly, grabbed the broom from the corner where he'd put it last night and started sweeping.

Hayden Lucht and Jared arrived about an hour later. She and Sid had swept, then vacuumed, brought Chiefy in, and got her food and water set up.

Sid leaned down and kissed her softly. "See you later. How about I bring you some lunch?"

"That would be nice. Are you sure you don't want me to bring you lunch?"

"Nope. I've got this." He nodded to Jared and Hayden, "See you guys later."

They both waved or nodded and kept on working.

Jared stood. "Grace, we'll need to replace two of these floorboards. They're soft and not able to be fixed as they are."

"Okay. Do you need something from me?"

"Nope, we just have to pull the floor back to this point, replace the boards and put the floor back in. It'll look like deconstruction for some time, but we'll have it finished today and the glass will be here this afternoon for the windows, so we'll get that fixed before we leave today."

She smiled at them. "You guys are a godsend. I don't know what I'd do without you both here."

Jared chuckled. "No worries. Dad said to make sure we took care of you and we are."

She'd make sure to tell Sid what Quinn said. He barely knew her, but Sid was his friend and they clearly stuck together, no matter what the task.

Grace painted her cabinet doors. They were all over the counters, the kitchen table, the stove, any surface she could lay a cabinet door, she did. But, the guys played music softly in the living room, they chatted about nothing in particular as they worked, and Chiefy was content to lay in her bed in the kitchen. She hadn't slept much last night, so she was a tired girl today. So was Grace.

The door opened and Sid entered with bags of food. "Hey guys. I brought you all lunch. Wash up, we'll eat. Jared glanced her way. She smiled and pointed down the hall.

She looked around and shrugged. "I don't have a surface for us to set the food on."

Sid grinned. "I've got it taken care of. Hang on." He set the bags of food on the coffee table, which was pushed up to the wall and stepped outside.

The door opened a few moments later and Sid carried in a long folding table. "I got this from Jace."

He unfolded it in the living room and set the food on it.

"Bring your kitchen chairs in here."

Grace carried the first wooden chair into the living room as Sid unpacked the bags of food, which smelled amazing.

He handed out sodas for everyone, and paper plates.

Jared and Hayden entered the living room with clean hands and sat across from her and Sid.

Jared grinned. "What are we eating?"

Sid laughed. "This morning Jace tried a chorizo recipe on Grace and me and we enjoyed it so much he decided to try out another one. These are chorizo tacos. Lime sauce, coleslaw topping, and lettuce. He wants to know what you all think of the food so you'll need to give me an honest opinion."

Hayden built the biggest taco she'd ever seen and shoved a good portion of it into his mouth. He chewed the best he could and finally swallowed then shook his head once, "Damn, that was great."

Sid chuckled and built his own taco and so did she. But nowhere near as big as Hayden's.

She bit into her taco and it was delicious. Simply fantastic.

"Jace has a hit with these tacos." Jared mumbled with a mouthful of food.

Sid nodded. "Agreed."

Jared built his second and devoured it just as fast as his first. They had worked hard today.

After she'd had two tacos she asked Sid, "Did the bikers come by the Garage today?"

"Yeah. One is sitting there right now. I asked Coop to lock up for lunch and he did. He went home to eat."

Hayden shook his head as he built his third taco. "Those bikers are a pain in the ass. My parents own the Grocery Store and they've been causing trouble in there almost daily. Dad has kicked them out now, and they sit outside on their bike trying to scare the patrons as they come in."

Sid asked, "Is it working?"

"Not really. They don't know us Florida people aren't scaredy cats like some of those city slickers."

Grace chuckled and tidied up her area, tossing the plate and napkins into the garbage can on the floor behind her.

Hayden continued. "They've also caused trouble at my girlfriend's hair salon on Main Street. One biker's old lady came in and wanted a haircut without an appointment. No one had time to do her hair, so she walked over to the retail shelves and knocked all the products off of one shelf. Then left. Now they drive by every hour or so and rev up their engines to disturb the salon patrons."

"That's terrible. I sure wish the police had the authority to do something about them. I guess they don't have the right to though."

Jared finished up his third taco. "Someone has to go to the city council."

Jace mentioned that too. Grace thought about that for a minute. "What has to be done at the city council?"

Sid turned and looked at her and grinned. "I can see your wheels turning."

"Well, I wonder what has to be done."

Jared balled up his napkin and paper plate. "I guess you have to go before the council during a meeting and ask for the municipal code of conduct of police and authorities to be amended to allow police to restrict troublemakers from coming into town."

Jared stood and rubbed his belly. "Thanks for lunch, Sid. Tell Jace, it was fantastic."

Sid laughed. "I will."

Hayden stood and threw his paper plate and napkin away, slurped down the last of his soda and tossed it all in the garbage.

Grace went to the kitchen to get a clean cloth to wipe Jace's table down. After wiping it, Sid folded it back up and kissed her lips once. He looked into her eyes. "I'll be back to take you and Chiefy to supper at the Sandbar if you like."

"I'd love that. Chiefy would too."

25

S id arrived at the garage to find Coop sweeping up glass. His heart dropped in his chest when he saw what those fucking bikers did.

He hopped out of his truck and rushed to help Coop. "Hey there, what happened?"

He knew what happened, but just in case he was wrong he wanted Coop to tell him. "Someone tossed three bricks through the windows."

Sid pulled his phone out and called the police.

"Don't go calling the police now."

"Gotta do it Coop. They need to know just how much damage those bikers are causing around town."

He got ahold of the dispatch operator and told her where he was and what happened and she replied in a tired voice. "I'll get someone over there as soon as I can, but they're dealing with problems at William's Hardware."

"Oh boy. These bikers sure are causing us a bunch of trouble."

"I didn't tell you it was the bikers."

"But it was, right?"

She let out a heavy sigh. "It seems so."

"Damn. Well, I'll be here when they can come down."

He finished his call and saw Coop pull up a chair from in front of the garage and sit down. His faded eyes locked on his and they stared at each other for a long time. Sid began to wonder what was going on with this old guy. "You got something on your mind?"

His stomach twisted. He'd caused all of this by not working with those bikers. Coop would probably ask him not to come back.

Coop sat back and rested his arms on the chair. He sat like that, still as can be for a moment then he nodded. "I'm too old for this shit, Sid. I come in to work here because the little woman gets on my nerves if I'm home all day. She wants me to do this and that and some more. If I'm home, I just want to enjoy my home. I don't want to work all the time, so I kept the Garage. But, what I realize is time is short. I'm old enough to be your father. My kids are grown and gone and my grandchildren are grown and gone too. All of them off doing something they want to do for a living. I have great kids and grandkids. None of them have been in trouble. All of them got good grades and played in sports."

He stopped a moment and as Sid was about to respond, Coop continued. "I've done good in my life. It's time someone else did good in their life. I'm offering for you to buy this place, Sid. The land, building, and every-thing in it. I'll give you a good deal and I'll even stop by once in a while and have a soda with you."

Sid stared for a long time. "You want me to buy the Garage?"

Coop nodded. "I do. I think you like it here. You straightened up my mess of tools, you sweep up every day and I've not seen anyone as good as you with a wrench in a long-damned time. I think you'll make a good living here. I have. I've filled a bank so to speak. Expenses are low, I don't have to advertise, and if you're good to people in town, they'll be loyal to you. I've seen you. You're loyal. Your friends are good friends and you've all been through a lot together. I know they'd love to have you here permanently."

Sid grinned. "You've been speaking to my friends?"

Coop shrugged. "Gotta know who I'm offering my garage to."

Sid took a deep breath and looked at the garage. He tilted his head up and looked at the faded sign - *GARAGE*. He chuckled.

"You could change the name of course. But, people will likely still call it the Garage. It's been that way for more than seventy years."

Sid looked at Coop and grinned. "You aren't that old."

"No. My pappy owned this garage before me. I grew up here though."

"What would you do about your wife nagging you to do things?"

"I'll just ignore her."

Sid burst out laughing. Coop chuckled a bit too.

His heart hammered in his chest. He liked it here. He felt at home here. He had friends here. And Grace. She was here. He'd met an amazing woman here.

"Can I speak to Grace first and let you know?"

Coop smiled. "You can."

He moved closer to Coop and reached down to shake the older man's hand. "Thanks, Coop. I appreciate that you're willing to sell this place to me."

Coop laughed. "I didn't even tell you what I want for it."

Sid laughed. "No, you didn't. What would you like for it?"

"I'd like you to pay me ten thousand dollars. And, always have a place for me to putter around if the little woman gets on my nerves."

Sid's eyes rounded. "That's not much for all of this, Coop. Your tools are likely worth more than that."

Coop shrugged. "Yeah. But, I told you I've made money. When I bought this place from my dad I paid ten thousand dollars. Granted ten grand back then was different than it is today. But, as I said, I've made money here and done good. I just want my investment back and a place to hide once in a while."

Sid nodded. He filled his lungs with air and tried to stop his body from shaking. This could be a game changer for him.

A squad car pulled into the lot and Sid turned to speak to the police officers on duty today. Then, he was going to beg off and go talk to Grace.

26

Grace stepped onto the porch with Chiefy to let her do her business. She heard a vehicle drive down the road and smiled when she saw Sid's truck. Then her brows bunched as she wondered why he was back so soon.

She moved to the grass with Chiefy, but her attention was on Sid. He pulled the truck to a stop in the driveway and when he exited, he had a grin on his face. That made her heartbeat return to a normal rhythm.

"Hi, gorgeous."

She chuckled. "Hi, yourself, handsome."

He stopped in front of her and kissed her lips, then said, "Can we have a little talk?"

"Sure." Her stomach twisted slightly. They hadn't had any heavy talks so she couldn't even dream what this meant.

"So, a couple of things. First, when I got back to the Garage, Coop was sweeping up glass. The bikers tossed bricks into the windows."

"Oh no. Is he alright?"

"Yes. He wasn't there. He came back from lunch to the mess."

"Okay. Well, I'm glad he's alright. How do you know it was the bikers?"

"One of the bikers sat across the street watching all morning. As soon as Coop left, the windows were broken and guess who isn't watching the Garage right now. No concrete evidence, but we know who's been causing all the trouble in town!"

"True."

"Anyway, he asked me if I wanted to buy the Garage."

Her heartbeat increased and she swallowed to wet her throat. What did this mean? Well, she knew what it meant, but...

"What did you say?"

"I said I wanted to talk to you."

Her eyes widened and she tilted her head. "Me?" She swallowed. "Why do you need to talk to me about it?"

Money? Her mind sped up and things popped in and out of her mind. He wouldn't ask her for money, his friends had plenty.

He motioned to the step on the deck. "Let's take a seat."

She sat down and Chiefy sniffed the area around the bottom of the deck. Sid turned to face her, took her hand in his and stared into her eyes.

"It was the first thing that popped into my head. I want to talk to Grace about this. I know we're new. But, Grace, I have never met anyone like you. I want to stay in your life and I want you in mine. I hadn't decided to move here until today, but I'd like to move here and buy the Garage. I'd like us to spend more time, all the time we can together. How does that make you feel?"

She let out a breath and chuckled. "I'd love that too. I didn't know where this was going."

He chuckled. "I'm sorry. I know this is all out of the blue. But, I was surprised that Coop asked me to buy the place and he's offering me the deal of a lifetime. But, if you didn't see us moving forward at all I won't stay here. It would be too hard to see you all the time and not be able to be with you. Talk to you. Spend time with you."

Chiefy licked his cheek and he laughed. "And Chiefy of course."

Grace swallowed and her hands shook slightly. A few months ago the thought of a relationship would have sent her packing up to go somewhere else. But, she'd never met anyone like Sid and...the realization that she wanted to spend more time with him slammed into her chest with a force.

"I want to spend more time with you too. I'm..." She took a deep breath. "I'm shocked, but happy and..." She cleared her throat. "Excited that you'll be here permanently."

He kissed her lips. His deep brown eyes stared into hers for a long time. His voice was a bit raspy when he spoke. "I never dreamed I'd find someone I'd want to spend time with. I never dreamed I'd meet a woman like you. Never. Dreamed."

Her eyes welled with tears. They came fast, her nose tingled and she sniffed. She swallowed. "Wow. Me too."

He kissed her lips again, this time he took his time. His tongue slipped between her lips and his hands held her head gently. They kissed sweetly, fully. His lips were so soft against hers. He was a fantastic kisser. His mouth formed to hers perfectly. She'd never been kissed as sweetly as Sid kissed her. She'd never craved kisses from anyone, even her ex, like she craved Sid's kisses. And, he kissed her often. Sweet little pecks. Longer kisses. Some in-between. But, he took the time to kiss her often and she liked it.

Chiefy licked her cheek and Sid's fingers. He chuckled and touched his forehead to hers.

She got her breathing under control as a truck pulled up to the front of the house. Quinn chuckled as he walked toward them. She could feel her cheeks heat up.

"Shouldn't you be at the Garage?" He jabbed.

Sid stood and shook his friend's hand, then hugged him. "Well, soon I'll be the owner and I'll come and go as I want."

Grace stood as Sid told Quinn about Coop offering him the Garage. Quinn hugged his friend and congratulated him. Grace watched the two men in conversation and thought how nice it was that they had this beautiful friendship.

Quinn finally addressed her. "Hello, Grace. I brought the glass for your windows so Jared and Hayden can get it installed. Are they doing a good job for you?"

"Oh, they're great. Come in and see the work they're doing. It's wonderful. I can't thank you enough for this and if I can pay you anything for the help, please let me know."

Quinn waved his hand in dismissal. "Sid's been my friend for more than twenty years. I'm happy to help out him or his friends. It's the least I can do."

Her chest heated and she glanced at Sid to see him staring at her. He had the most beautiful smile on his face. He was certainly a handsome man. But, more than that, he was a good man. Luck had sure shined down on her.

27

id kissed Grace's lips and petted Chiefy before climbing in the truck to tell Coop he was going to buy the Garage. He couldn't remember a time when he felt so happy about the future. He had purpose now. He had Grace. And, he'd have his own business. And, right here in town with his two best friends who also owned businesses. So, he'd have sounding boards and friends to bounce ideas off of. And, again, he had Grace. That was the most exciting part of his future. She was exciting.

He pulled into the Garage parking area. Coop was inside working on an older truck that had been brought in earlier today. He looked up as Sid parked, wiped his hands on a rag hanging from his pocket and waited for Sid to come closer.

"Did you talk to your girl?"

"I did."

Coop nodded but said nothing. Sid's heartbeat was wild in his chest. He was barely able to contain his excitement. "I'd like to buy the Garage from you, Coop."

Coop smiled. The wrinkles on his face, scrunched a bit more, the creases around his eyes deepened. "I figured."

Sid laughed. "You did?"

"Yeah. That girl is smitten with you. She looks at you like my missus looks at me. She's besotted."

Sid shook his head and furrowed his brows. Did she? He hadn't noticed. Likely because he was always staring at her. He probably looked like a sick cow.

Coop laughed. "You look at her that way too. Just so you know."

"I don..." He cocked his head to the side and stared at the old man. His grin said it all. He was a man of years who'd seen and done things Sid had yet to experience. He was a man who saw things others didn't because he watched people. He wanted to ask if he looked like that sick cow he'd imagined, but didn't want to hear the answer.

Sid nodded. "Thank you for pointing that out. I hope I always look at her that way."

Coop chuckled. He tucked his thumbs in the front pockets of his bib overalls. "You gonna rename her?"

Sid's brows bunched. Grace? Why would he...then he realized Coop meant the Garage. He grinned at the old man and nodded. "Miracle Garage."

The old man laughed out loud, slapped his hips, and nodded. "That works."

He stepped forward and held his hand out. "I'll have my lawyer draw up the papers. When do you want to make this official?"

Sid shrugged. "As soon as you can get the paperwork done. I have the money in the bank. It's no problem there."

Coop nodded. "We'll shoot for next week."

Coop turned to finish working on the truck. He said over his shoulder, "What are you going to do about those bikers?"

Sid thought for a moment. He wasn't sure. Not yet, but maybe he and Grace would try to work with the city council and see what they could do. But, they'd do it together.

"I'm not a hundred percent sure at this point." He opened a shop rag, dropped some tools in it to take out to the bike and rolled them up in the rag.

As he moved toward the door, Coop nodded. "Don't let them win."

He nodded as he looked around the garage. He'd be damned if he let them win. He was finally, finally, realizing his dreams. Funny thing is he didn't even know these were his dreams a few weeks ago. But, he'd stumbled on this small close-knit town. He was near his friends. He'd own his own business which would help him fully become part of this community. He had a place he felt he really belonged.

He sucked in a lungful of air, turned slowly and meandered toward the Knucklehead. He felt giddy and light as air. He couldn't wait to celebrate with Grace tonight. He couldn't wait...

Where would they spend tonight? The sound of a motorcycle reached his ears. He watched the street, as a biker pulled to a stop about three blocks down. He sat back on his parked bike, nonchalantly, but watching the Garage. Sid wondered if there was one sitting down the road from Grace's.

He pulled his phone out to call her when Jace pulled

to a stop in front of the garage. "Hey, there, grease monkey."

Sid chuckled. "That's me."

"I just heard the good news. You're now a business owner in Blossom Springs?"

"Well, unofficially. Next week it'll be official."

"Perfect. Then, I'll invite you and Grace to our little business association. We like to stay on top of all things that have to do with the commerce of our town. Meetings are every first Monday of the month."

"We'll be there."

"Where are you two staying tonight? I see you still have a tail. Grace has one too."

"I was just thinking about that. And, since I'll be here permanently, I should look for a little place of my own to call home. If you hear of any good places, let me know."

Jace laughed. "I've got the perfect place for you and Grace and Chiefy."

Sid's heartbeat kicked up. They hadn't talked about living together. Just continuing to see each other. Before he could respond, Jace said. "I'll set up a showing for this evening."

He didn't wait for a response, he took off driving down Main Street toward the Sandbar. Sid took in a deep breath. Things were moving fast. He waited for the usual tingling to happen just before he had a panic attack. He knelt in front of the Knucklehead so he wouldn't fall if he got dizzy. He waited some more. Then, he realized, no panic attacks were coming. He wasn't at all panicked about any of this. He was excited.

He blew out a breath, unwrapped the tools he'd pulled from the garage to work on the Knucklehead and with a smile on his face, he started pulling the starter off the bike. He'd kick off early tonight to speak with Grace about the little house and what her thoughts were on moving in together.

28

Grace closed and locked the door after Jared and Hayden left for the day. Glancing at her watch she noted the time at three-thirty. She had a fresh coat of paint on the cabinets in the kitchen, and they were drying. The flooring was finished. Her windows repaired. And, there was still a biker watching her place. She took a deep breath and decided to take the time to do some research.

Pulling her laptop from its case, she sat on the sofa. As soon as it booted up, she typed in Blossom Springs City Council. As the screen populated, she took a deep dive into the world of the Blossom Springs government and its workings.

After a while, Chiefy began to pace at the door and whine so Grace closed the lid on her laptop and stood just as someone knocked. She jumped. She hadn't heard anyone pull into the driveway. Moving to the window, which offered her a view of the front door, she saw Sid standing outside. His posture was straight, his handsome face a pleasure to see.

She opened the door and stepped back as Sid entered. He kissed her lips, petted Chiefy, and looked at the windows.

"Everything looks great."

"They've done a wonderful job." She smiled, "Did you take off work early today?"

His brows furrowed. "No, I meant to, but I ended up working until five o'clock. Coop started showing me some things in the shop and how he handles the air conditioning when it acts up, and how he keeps track of inventory."

She glanced at her watch. Her eyes rounded. "Oh, my goodness. I've been on the computer for an hour and a half. I didn't even realize."

Sid chuckled. Grace turned to the sofa and pulled up her laptop. She sat in the same spot she'd recently vacated, and Sid sat next to her.

"I've been researching how to approach the city council about the bikers and their nuisance behavior. Officer Moody told me the police can't do anything until the bikers cause trouble. They can't run them out of town. They take their orders from their chief, who has to follow what the city council has written a law on and approved. Right now, to get in front of the board to discuss this, you have to call and submit your agenda item and then wait for the next meeting. At which time, they'll discuss your agenda item. The thing is, after that, they'll put it on the agenda to discuss how to handle it. Then, a law will have to be written, if the council decides it's important enough to do so. Then, it'll go through approvals, revisions, and that whole process. I'd guess about a year. Who knows what will happen in a year!"

He grinned at her. "You've done a great job researching this."

She smiled and stared into his eyes. "Thank you."

"So, we have to come up with another plan?"

"There is another way. We can ask for an emergency meeting and an expedited solution. But, we need a petition with five hundred signatures, which is nearly one-quarter of the population of Blossom Springs. How will we get that many signatures to ask for this emergency meeting?"

Sid leaned back as he stared at her computer. He slowly leaned to the side and pulled his phone from his back pocket. Without another word to her, he tapped his phone and put it on speaker.

Jace chuckled. "Hey, buddy, what's up?"

"In order to get the city council to hold an emergency board meeting and an expedited solution, we need a petition with five hundred signatures of Blossom Springs residents. Feel like holding a party?"

Jace replied, "Fuck, yeah." Rustling could be heard as it sounded like Jace was walking through the restaurant. "So, two things. I need about a week to get the word out. Between regulars here, staff, and social media, we can reach a ton of people. And, I just heard today that Jami Hart and the Hurricanes are back in town. If I can talk them into performing, we'll get a shit ton of people here and can get those signatures you need."

Sid chuckled and winked at her. "That's perfect. Tell me what I need to do to help get the word out."

"Let me put some things together. I'll give you an update tomorrow."

Oh, this was too good to be true. They'd get their petition if not completely signed, they'd have a fantastic start on it.

"Sounds great. What's the second thing?"

"Ah, oh yeah. You can see the house at six o'clock. I'll text you the address. I have someone opening it up for you to see it."

"What do you mean you have someone opening it up?"

Jace laughed. "Oh yeah. I own the house. I bought it when I first got here. Then the Governor's Mansion became available and I moved after it was remodeled. My house has been sitting empty. I've kept it up though. Pest control and my cleaning lady goes in every two weeks just to dust and clean."

Sid chuckled. "You are full of surprises."

"I suppose. You'll like the house. It's just out of town. Quiet. It sits up on the bluff. You can see the water, though there isn't any access to it from up there. But, its views are stunning."

Sid turned his head and their eyes met. He smiled so perfectly she could have swooned. Literally, he was just that handsome. But, this whole house thing was a puzzle.

"Sounds good. Send me the address. We'll check it out."

"Okay. Talk to you later."

The call ended and Sid turned to face her. He cocked his left leg so it laid on the sofa, bent at the knee. "So, since I'm buying the Garage I need a more permanent place to live. I mentioned it to Jace and as you heard, he has a place available. I'd love for you and Chiefy to come with me and see it."

Butterflies took flight in her tummy and her throat dried. She swallowed to wet it, then took a deep breath. "Okay."

"You seem hesitant."

She chuckled, more out of nervousness than anything else. "I'm happy to look at it with you. But, it's your decision where you live."

He leaned forward and kissed her lips. "I'd like your opinion."

The drive to Jace's house was picturesque. The road curved up the bluff looking over the water. It wasn't far from Grace's houses. That was a bonus. The road curved slightly and as they pulled into the driveway, the view of the water below was breathtaking. The sun was beginning to set, though it wouldn't completely set for another hour and a half, but it was lower in the sky. The brightness of the day was now tinged with an orange hue.

Grace sighed. "This is stunning."

He smiled as he watched the movement of the water. A couple of boats were out on the water fishing, the scene nearly picture-perfect. The house was a ranch-style home, sprawling along the bluff, offering a scenic view of the area and water below.

A truck pulled in behind his truck and he took a deep breath and looked over at Grace. "Ready?"

"Yes. Should I bring Chiefy in or leave her out here?"

Sid shrugged and Chiefy sniffed his ear then licked his

cheek. He could almost swear she knew they were talking about leaving her out here. He chuckled. "She can come in. Jace said so earlier today."

"He did?"

"Yes. Full confession, he said this would be the perfect house for the three of us."

He stared into her eyes. Worried she'd bolt, or think he had been trying to trick her into something. He wasn't. He never wanted to trick her into anything. He wanted her to want to be with him and for only one reason. Because she wanted to be. Maybe someday she'd fall in love with him. That thought made his heart race. His throat dried and he swallowed a few times.

"Okay. I..."

"Hey. No pressure. Not from me. Not from Jace. He merely said this house would be perfect for the three of us, and I said we hadn't talked about that at all."

She inhaled deeply and let it out slowly. Her blue eyes were clear and bright and so insanely beautiful it left him speechless. "Okay."

"You sure?"

He took her left hand in his right hand and squeezed. "But, if you think for one minute that you'd enjoy living here with me, please let me know. I'm open to you and Chiefy being here. Not only open to it, I'd love it."

Grace swallowed and the person in the truck behind them tapped on Sid's window.

Sid turned around to see Quinn grinning ear to ear. "Hey."

Sid opened his door and stepped down. "Jace didn't tell me you were the one showing us the house." He hugged his friend.

"I offered this afternoon when he also asked me to check on the fascia on the water side of the house. He thought it looked loose in a couple of spots."

"Sounds good. Let me help Grace with Chiefy."

"I'll go unlock the house."

Sid hurried around the truck and opened Grace's door. She looked into his eyes as she stepped down, a soft smile on her face. He leaned down and kissed her lips briefly. "No pressure."

"Okay."

He opened the back door and grabbed Chiefy's leash. She jumped from the truck and immediately her nose began sniffing the ground as they walked to meet up with Quinn.

"Hey, Grace, it's nice to see you again." Quinn leaned forward and quickly hugged Grace.

"It's nice to see you too," she replied.

Her eyes turned quickly to his after Quinn hugged her and he got the feeling she was worried. He placed his hand at the nape of her neck and squeezed lightly. She tilted her head up and looked into his eyes again, a soft smile on her face.

Quinn opened the front door and stepped aside for them to enter.

They stepped into a small foyer, a round table in the middle with a vase of flowers sitting on it. To the right was a study, to the left the living room. Quinn moved to the living room.

"Tell me if you'd prefer to walk around and see things for yourself or if you want me along. I can tell you, over the years I've worked on this house a few times, before Jace bought it. It's well-built and the work that has been done by me or my crew was cosmetic and nothing that anyone would worry about. For instance, when Jace bought the house, he wanted the hardwood floors redone. I also did some work in the kitchen. We added a couple of cabinets, hand crafting them to match the existing cabinets."

Grace smiled. "You and your crew do custom hand-crafted work?"

"Yes ma'am. We do it all."

Sid glanced down at Grace. "What do you say, should we meander about by ourselves?"

"Sure. Chiefy will follow us around without hanging on to her leash. She never wants to be left out."

Quinn chuckled. "I'll leave you to it then. I'll step out of the kitchen door and check that fascia for Jace. I'll make sure the door is closed so Chiefy doesn't get out."

Sid nodded and grinned at his friend. "Thanks, Quinn."

They stepped into the living room which had a nice view of the water below. Large picture windows to the side allowed light to filter in and the view to be seen. The hard-wood floors were in perfect shape.

Grace stood at the window and looked out at the water. Sid stood next to her for a few quiet moments.

He decided to let her think about this on her own and he moved into the entryway, then down the short hallway which led to a kitchen and dining room. Both with spec-tacular views of the water below. Large windows again allowed the outside in.

Grace followed him into the kitchen and stood facing the cabinets, which were beautiful gleaming oak. The countertops were granite in a soft caramel color with swirls of dark brown and gold flecks in it. She ran her hand over the smooth granite, and he saw her take a deep breath.

She turned and looked at the gas stove, which was newer, stainless steel. There was also a matching refrigerator, dishwasher, and a microwave above the stove. It was stunning.

He glanced into the dining area, the breakfast nook sat in a little cove with benches built around it, the oak table matching the cabinets sat in the middle. It was cozy and homey and so far, he liked the house a lot. The kitchen door to the outside was between the breakfast nook and kitchen, the dining room off to the left of the nook.

Grace's voice was soft when she said, "This is simply stunning."

"It certainly is."

They moved together, Chiefy close behind, out of the kitchen and down a hallway to the right, and a row of doors. Actually, only three doors to the left, the water side, and two doors to the right, the driveway side of the house as it sat.

The first bedroom was smaller, and looked as though it was an office. A large section of cabinets painted white, stood against the far wall and a desk was built into the corner, in front of the windows looking out on the water.

Grace stepped into the room and chuckled. "This is a Murphy bed."

Sid's brows furrowed. "A what?"

"Murphy bed. Look." She pulled the doors open and then tugged on a strap hanging onto a frame. A wooden frame and mattress lowered slowly to the floor. "That is so cool."

Sid chuckled. "I've never seen one of those before."

"They're great for a dual-purpose room like this. How fantastic."

She lifted the frame and he assisted to tuck them back into the cabinet. It moved easily and her smile was genuine as she watched the doors close.

She beamed at him. "That's pretty cool."

"It is."

The view in this room was as fantastic as the other rooms and whoever built this house did so with the views in mind.

He turned to move along the hallway to the next room and found it was a nice size bedroom with a queen size bed and dresser inside. The hardwood floors were the same throughout the house and in immaculate shape. The view, again, stunning.

Finally, the last room toward the end of the hall had to be the main bedroom. He entered the room and his heart felt...at peace. That was the best way to describe it. The room was large. A king size bed was across from the windows, situated so he could lay in bed and stare out the windows at the view below. Across from the water were palm trees and a field.

He sat on the bed, near the pillows, and gazed out of the windows, picturing the mornings here. But, in his mind's eye, he saw Grace here too, and Chiefy licking his face. This was a house for all of them, not just him.

He watched Grace as she sat on the other side of the bed and stared out the window, a wistful look on her face.

"What do you think, Grace?"

She turned her head, her lips parted perfectly into a dazzling smile. "I think it's perfect."

He took a deep breath. Fear gripped him tightly as he opened his mouth to ask her the important question, and he couldn't say it. He cleared his throat and swallowed.

Grace chuckled. "I could live here."

His heartbeat increased so fast his head jerked. "You could?"

"I could." She smiled. "This is a gorgeous house, Sid. I had no idea it was here. No idea this bluff existed. But, wow, what a view, and on top of that, this place is stunning."

"It is. But, I was just thinking I can't picture myself here without you and Chiefy here. I see all of us in this house, not just me. This isn't a house for only one person."

Grace swallowed. "It's a big step."

"It is. But, here's the thing Grace. We're both in our fifties. We've both been hurt before. We've both suffered through divorces. And, we've lived on our own. I knew the moment I met you, you were someone I wanted to get to know. Every minute I spend with you is precious to me. Why don't we try living together. You still have your bungalows. You can start renting the first one out soon, you'll be here. Then you can work on the second one. And, I don't think it will happen, but if we figure we don't want to be together anymore, you can move back to one of your bungalows."

Her throat moved as she swallowed, her face still gorgeous, but didn't show the emotion she must be feeling. His heart though, was beating so hard, it was uncomfortable.

Grace turned her head toward him. "How are you so sure?"

He took in a deep breath. "At this point in my life, I've been through so much. I'm not a young man anymore. I don't have pie-in-the-sky ideals. I've met a woman who has a good head on her shoulders, a great dog, and to be honest, how you take care of Chiefy says a lot about who you are as a person. I know enough in my heart that I don't want this opportunity with you to just float away. I know in my heart that we're compatible. I know that what we've both been through has molded us into people who have suffered, but still want what life has to offer. And, I know I will do my best to make sure you are happy."

She smiled. A genuine, beautiful, soft smile. "What I've learned is I have to be happy on my own, not expect another person to make me happy. But, I believe I've figured that out for myself. I'm happy to make my own living and live on my own terms. To not be controlled by another human, never again."

His stomach twisted slightly. "I'd never try to control you, Grace."

She leaned over and laid her hand over his. "I didn't mean that. But, I thought it should be said."

"This is why I have such strong feelings for you, Grace. You're level-headed and willing to talk through the unsaid things."

"Well, I'm glad you feel that way. So, here's the biggest thing. I don't know what Jace is asking for this place, but I can't imagine it's inexpensive. What is your plan as it pertains to me?"

"Do you mean do I expect you to pay for this? Or half of it? Or anything?"

She shrugged a shoulder. "Well...yeah."

"No. I have money. I'm not a multi-millionaire, but I've lived simply, and saved all my life. My parents passed and left me with enough money to never have to worry about where I live or how I live. I don't have kids. And, I don't need to live in the lap of luxury. But, this place feels like home to me. Especially if you're here."

"Then, I should say, I don't have a ton of money. I'm making it. I know my little bungalows will be profitable and I hope to buy more."

"Then, I think this is the perfect fit for both of us."

He leaned over and kissed her lips. Then, he kissed her again. He touched his forehead to hers. "Move here with me."

30

Grace's heartbeat came in rhythmic thuds in her chest. She liked Sid. Probably more than like, but it was soon. And, she was scared. Terrified is more like it. She was terrified. She'd left her bad marriage, and it was nothing short of a miracle that she came out as good as she did. Her ex fought her every step of the way. He wanted to control everything. Luckily, she had a great attorney who had seen men like this before, and she let him have it with both barrels. Her ex had to pay her for half of the house, they didn't have credit card debt, thank goodness, but he did have to pay for his own bills that he'd piled up along the way. So, she left with enough money to buy her little bungalows, fix them up, and then put a nice down payment on the next ones as soon as she could see fit.

She stared into Sid's deep brown eyes. She felt like she could see him in them. Really see him. He didn't look away from her. He didn't hide from her. He didn't hide his illness, though it would be impossible to, since that's how they met. But, since that first day, he didn't hide anything from her. He fessed up in the driveway about Jace, before they came in to look at the house. So, she knew where his head was the entire time.

His deep voice floated over her like a warm blanket. "Tell me what you're thinking, Grace."

She took a deep breath. "I'm thinking I'm scared."

His fingers squeezed hers. "I understand that. How about if we leave this big decision for another time then?"

As he looked into her eyes, she saw earnestness. "I don't want to leave you hanging. This is an incredible opportunity for you."

He chuckled. "Oh, I'm buying the house. It's perfect. I like being away from town, but not too far. I can see coming home at night and relaxing on that porch out back, staring at the water like I do at the bungalow, but without all the people milling about. Just this sanctuary called home. In my mind I see you here clearly. But, what's important is that you see yourself here clearly."

Yes, that was true. That's what she needed to see. And, if she were honest with herself, she could see living here. It was absolutely a sanctuary. A place that worked like a balm on a tired soul. Home, he'd said home. She hadn't felt like she'd ever had a home. Not since she left her parent's home to go to college. Her life with her ex was always tumultuous. Everything was what he wanted. What he said. Where he wanted to go. She had little say in anything, including the house they lived in. He decided where they'd live.

"Can we go out and see the front porch?"

He chuckled. "I'd like that. I only had a glimpse from the window."

She stood and Chiefy jumped up from the rug she'd been laying on and it struck Grace that Chiefy felt comfortable here too. She'd laid down on a rug without whining or pacing.

As Grace reached the bedroom door she turned and stared out the window at the sun, now lowering itself into the water, its orange burst about to extinguish for the evening.

Sid's hand found hers and she wrapped her fingers with his as they walked the hallway to the kitchen. As they stepped into the kitchen, the beauty of the room and the warmth of the man standing next to her felt like a warm blanket. She felt peaceful here.

Sid bent and grabbed Chiefy's leash, then opened the back door for her. The wooden porch was covered, and enclosed with windows, which someone had opened, maybe Quinn. The room was inviting, and they didn't have to slap at mosquitos as they took in the landscape. Sid led them to a tan, L-shaped sofa, which allowed them to relax and enjoy. As soon as they sat together, his arm wrapped around her shoulders and she laid her head on his shoulder. His breathing was even, his presence comforting. She didn't feel the nervous energy she used to feel with her ex. She was always afraid she was doing something wrong and he'd criticize her for it. All evening long. Here, she felt truly relaxed.

Birds flew over the water, one of them swooped down and picked a fish from the water. Chiefy barked and her tail wagged as it flew past their view, looking like it was coming to offer them food.

Chiefy sat down and stared out the windows just as they did.

"I want to live here with you, Sid. If you're sure you want us here."

He kissed the top of her head and squeezed her shoulders. "I've been sure about many things in my life, Grace. I've been unsure too. I'm absolutely sure that I'd love for you and Chiefy to live here with me."

She swallowed the lump in her throat. Her nose tingled as tears threatened. She sat next to Sid as she was and let the feelings flow over her. A tear slipped from her eye and landed on his shirt.

After she felt she could talk without crying, she said. "I've never known peace like this before."

"Me either, sweetheart."

Chiefy finally laid down on the rug in the Florida room, flopped to her side and closed her eyes. She was at peace here too. That said a lot.

31

On Friday, two days from his decision to buy Jace's house and Grace agreeing to move in with him, Sid opened a checking and savings account at the local bank. He worked with the personal rep there to transfer his money from his bank back home, to this bank. He'd go back in a week or two, give notice on his condo, and pack up his belongings. He'd need his furniture here and he and Grace would figure out what pieces to keep and what to get rid of. They'd decided some of the pieces of furniture Grace had would fit in the house and they'd be making that move soon.

Leaving the bank, Sid headed straight to the Garage. A biker was already in position, but Sid nodded and waved at him before nonchalantly entering the garage. Coop was sitting behind the counter in the reception area, writing on a note pad.

"Good morning. You're hard at work at something not car or truck related I see." He quipped.

"It's car and truck related, but not physically. I'm writing down all the vendors I work with. The missus said I should do this and if you or Grace can email these folks and let them know you're the new contact here, that would help you out."

"Thank you, and thank the missus for me. That would be helpful indeed."

Coop laughed. "She's the brains of this operation."

Sid chuckled. "Any bricks tossed today?"

"Nope, but the day ain't over. And, I heard that the grocery store had another issue. A couple of them bikers decided to bring their motorcycles into the store and rev the engines. They filled the place with exhaust and left a few black marks on the floors on their way out of town."

"Why did they do that?"

"Apparently the store doesn't carry the kind of beer they like."

Sid shook his head. "They're pissing everyone off around here. If they don't like it here, they should move on."

"My feeling exactly." Coop's faded blue eyes stared into his. "Don't let them win, Sid."

"We're working on something to get rid of them."

"Good." Coop closed his notebook. "I'm going to let this percolate today. I'll remember more as the day goes on."

"Thanks, Coop." He started toward the garage area but stopped. "I'm buying a house."

"A house?" Coop barked. "Well aren't you settling down!"

"That I am."

Sid felt light as he assembled the tools for the Knucklehead. He turned to Coop, who had followed him out here. "I suppose I should start working on vehicles as they come in."

Coop laughed. "I was wondering when you'd get there!"

Sid laughed. "Next one that comes in is mine."

Coop chuckled and started working on an old farm truck brought in for new brakes. Sid carried his tools to the Knucklehead and started working.

His mind raced to Grace, the house, the stuff he had to do to close up his place, the Garage, all the things. But, he didn't feel overwhelmed. He felt excited.

A motorcycle pulled into the driveway, then a second one. The bikers got off their bikes and strutted toward Sid. He stood and waited for them to approach. The first man, who reminded him of Grizzly Adams - full beard in need of a trim, long hair, in need of a wash, burly build covered in tattoos and leather. That part wasn't Grizzly Adams, but the rest of him was.

"You the owner?"

"Yep."

"That so?"

"Yep."

"I hear you won't work for us exclusively."

"That's correct."

"Why not?"

"Because this garage has been part of this town for more than seventy years. It's a staple for the local towns-people and farmers. I'm not turning anyone away because I have to be exclusive to you or anyone else."

"I can burn this place to the ground."

"I can rebuild it."

They stared at each other for some time. He refused to back down. These assholes needed to be taught a lesson. They'd do it legally first, then if need be, he'd do it physically. They weren't going to ruin his new little slice of heaven.

"We'll be back."

Sid nodded but said nothing more. He waited where he was, staring at them as they prepared to leave; they backed their bikes out of the driveway and onto the street. As soon as they took off, he pulled his phone from his back pocket and called Grace.

"Hi," she cheerfully greeted.

"Hi, yourself."

"What's up?"

"Two bikers just came here to intimidate me. I'm warning you they may be coming down by you, I saw them turn that way."

"Yes, I hear them now." She took a deep breath and whooshed it from her lungs.

"Do you need me to come down there?"

"They've stopped and are speaking with the biker watching my place today."

He took a deep breath and started walking toward the footpath that led across Jace's place. "Grace. Do you need me to come there?"

"I...um...I'll just make sure all the doors and windows are locked up."

"Honey, I'm on my way. I'm taking the footpath, get ready for me at the back door."

"Sid, you don't..."

"Back door, babe."

He ended the call and began jogging. As soon as he arrived at Grace's he'd call Jace and let him know what was happening.

He knocked on the back door to Grace's place. Chiefy barked and Grace shushed her, though she barked again.

The locks clicked and he saw her face. It was nothing short of a shot in the arm. She always made him feel stronger.

He stepped inside. Turning he locked the door then walked to the front of the house and looked out the window. There they all sat. Three of them to scare one little woman. It pissed him off.

Grace stood back a few feet watching him. He turned and grinned at her. "They came to the Garage and threatened to burn it down if I didn't agree to be exclusive with them."

"Oh my god they are getting worse and worse. What did you say?"

"I told them I'd rebuild it."

Her smile said it all. "Good for you." She stepped closer. "How do you feel?"

"Strong. Determined to see them run out of town."

"Okay. Me too."

A week passed with much of the same going on. The bikers continued to watch them, but Grace and Sid continued to move forward with their plans. Sid bought the house on the bluff from Jace. It was an incredible deal and Sid loved that he'd purchased it from Jace.

Today, they were moving her sofa and bed into the house. Her bed was only a queen size bed, and since the house came with the large king bed that was there when they looked at it, her bed would go in the spare bedroom. She removed the sheets from her bed and dropped them in the laundry hamper to wash once they were at the house. Carrying the laundry basket to the living room she set it on the sofa and looked at her little place. She'd finished her work here and had put it on the short-term rental sites last night. Hopefully she'd have guests soon.

Sid entered the bungalow with Quinn, carrying tools. "Are you ready for me to take the bed apart?"

"Yes. I'll pull my clothes from the closet and dresser and put them in my car."

Quinn grinned. "Where are your guests going to sleep?"

She chuckled. "I have another bed being delivered today. The headboard is more of a beachy vibe and will fit the whole theme here much better."

"You've done a great job here, Grace."

"Thank you. It wouldn't be finished without Jared and Hayden helping me. So, thank you for offering your men to my project."

"Happy to help."

Quinn and Sid went to the bedroom and Grace packed up Chiefy's water and food bowl, the container of dog food, the pig ears she chewed on, and her bed. She placed them in the trunk of her car, waved at the bikers watching them, and went back inside.

They wouldn't be able to get close to the house, that was a bonus not to have to see them each night.

She entered the house and her phone rang. "Hello, this is Grace."

"Hey, Grace, it's Theresa from the Sandbar."

"Hi, Theresa, how can I help you?"

"Jace asked me to let you know that we have things all set for tonight. We'll have a table outside for you to take care of the petition. Hart & the Hurricanes will be here to play tonight, and we've all been promoting it on our socials. We should have a fantastic turnout."

"Thank you, Theresa. Sid and I will be down there early tonight to get set up."

"See you then."

Sid and Quinn entered the living room carrying the mattress. Sid asked, "We're ordering new dishes, right?"

"Yes. I have them ordered and they should be delivered today. Jace has everything set for tonight."

"Perfect."

They moved past her with the mattress and went out the door. She closed it behind them and prepared to take her clothes out to the car. She had plastic totes, which she'd moved here with, now filled with the clothing from the dresser. She picked up the first one and carried it to the living room. The other two totes held her clothes from her closet. She carried those to the living room as well just as Quinn and Sid came back inside.

Without a word they each carried a tote to her car. She grinned. Her heart felt full. She looked at Chiefy, "Ready to go, girl?"

Chiefy whined and followed her to the car without a leash on. She knew Grace was going somewhere and no way was she going to be left behind. Grace opened the back door and Chiefy jumped right in. Sid came over to the car with a grin on his face. Sweat dripped down his temples and his shirt was wet under his arms and his back was drenched. He leaned in gently and kissed her lips, then grinned. "I'll see you up there in a few minutes."

"Sounds good. I'll get to unpacking things so we can shower and get ready to be at the Sandbar by seven."

"Perfect. I'm going to need a shower."

She laughed. "Yeah, me too. But we won't have to deal with those guys watching the house tonight."

"Which reminds me, we have security."

"You mean Chiefy?"

He chuckled. "Well, she's our first line of security. Our second line is the cameras installed along the driveway and all around the house."

"Really? I didn't know that."

"Jace told me this morning. He gave me the codes." He

pulled a sheet of paper from his wallet. "I'll need those back."

She laughed. "Here, let's do this." She pulled her phone out and took a picture of the codes. "Do I need to do anything when I go up there?"

"No, they're turned off right now. But, I'll show you where everything is when I get up there."

"Okay." She stood on her toes and kissed his lips. "See you in a few minutes."

"Count on it."

Grace jumped in her car and started it up. The humidity was high today. She'd been sweating all morning as the door to the bungalow had been opened and closed over and over again. Plus all the packing.

She pulled onto Sunset Beach Road, and stayed left at the fork to their new private driveway/road, named Bluff Road. Just like most of the other places and roads here in Blossom Springs. She grinned as she turned up Bluff Road. The sound of a motorcycle behind her had Chiefy growling low. Glancing in her rearview mirror, she saw the biker follow her. After she turned onto Bluff Road, she watched to see if the biker would follow her. There was a sign at the bottom of the road that proudly boasted 'private property'. And still another one that read, "security cameras in use."

She hadn't noticed that before, but she was glad for it now. The biker stopped and she and Chiefy continued up to their new home. The only thing that made her stomach twist, was that her little bungalows didn't have security on them. They would be there like sitting ducks. Hopefully their party at the Sandbar tonight would get them the signatures they needed to ask the council to take action.

To date, the bikers had damaged several businesses,

continued to harass or stalk Sid, her, and she'd also heard they were doing the same thing to the gas station owner, Bodie. But, to everyone's credit, people weren't exactly caving to the pressure. They carried on with their business and repaired the damage. In one instance the same insurance company was involved for two separate businesses. There was talk that the insurance company might start looking into the bikers. But in actuality, they'd likely not do anything.

At the top of Bluff Road, Grace pulled to a stop in the space she'd been parking in since they'd begun to move things into the house. Chiefy whined in excited anticipation and Grace chuckled. "I'll hurry."

She opened Chiefy's door and her pup ran to her favorite spot to pee, then to the front door as Grace grabbed her supplies and carried them to the house.

Using the key Sid had given her, she unlocked the door and pushed it open with her butt as Chiefy burst through and excitedly ran to her spot in the kitchen where one of her beds laid. Yes, she had three beds in this house. She was a spoiled girl.

33

Sid saw the biker follow Grace to the new house and his blood began to boil. He and Quinn loaded the bed frame and a few of the totes that didn't fit in Grace's car into the trucks and took off toward the house. As soon as he reached Bluff Road, the biker was sitting across from the driveway, but on his cellphone. Sid wanted to lift his middle finger so damned bad. He'd settle for watching these assholes drive out of town. That would have to be enough.

He did make sure though, that the biker saw him staring at him. Yes, he and Grace knew they were watching, but it wouldn't stop them.

Taking a deep breath, he once again marveled at the drive up the bluff. It bent and turned on the way up and was as pretty as a picture. Never did he dream he'd live in a place like this.

Life was sure funny.

Grace stepped out of the front door and waved as she strode to her car and grabbed another tote. Her face glowed in the way women glow when they perspire. She had a dewy glow about her and she looked stunning in her khaki shorts and white tank top. She had her dark hair pulled back in a ponytail and it swished back and forth as she walked.

He pulled to a stop and pulled another tote from her car and followed her into the house. "Does this one go into the bedroom?"

She glanced at it and nodded. "It sure does."

He followed her down the hall, happily watching her ass sway.

Entering the bedroom his heart leapt once again. He loved this room. The past week they'd stayed between his place on the beach and Grace's place. Bikers be damned. So far they hadn't resorted to the arson they threatened, but it didn't mean it wouldn't escalate. He hoped they didn't have any idea what tonight's party was all about or they may just get very aggressive.

He set the tote down on top of another one and turned to head out and help Quinn bring in the spare bed. Grace stepped from the large walk-in closet and chuckled. "I've honestly never dreamed of living in a place like this."

"I know what you mean."

He kissed her lips quickly and hurried outside to help Quinn. Chiefy ran to him for a bit of affection, which he took the time to offer. He'd grown to love her. She was an incredible force in the house and she always watched out for him.

He scratched behind her ear, "I'm getting you some big ole' pig ears tomorrow girl."

Chiefy cocked her head to the side as if she understood and he chuckled. "You're a smart one."

He turned to the door and hustled to the truck to help Quinn.

After the last of the items were placed inside the house, Grace called from the kitchen. "I made sweet tea and sandwiches."

He and Quinn hustled to the kitchen like two starving cats. She laughed when they both stepped into the kitchen. "Oh, Lordy. You two are a sight. Sit at the breakfast nook and let me get you some food."

He shrugged and Quinn eagerly sat at the breakfast nook, both of them tired and sweaty from the heat and the day's work.

Quinn chuckled. "I don't work this hard at work."

Sid laughed. "We didn't even have to move much."

"That's a fact. Still, holy shit is it hot outside."

"Reminds me of being in Iraq."

"God that was a fire box. Sand blowing the skin off our bodies and the sun cooking us."

Grace brought them a pitcher of sweet tea and two glasses. Sid hurriedly poured Quinn some tea, then himself. The first few drinks were more like gulps. He refilled, so did Quinn and they both drank more. Grace giggled as she carried sandwiches to the table. "Sorry it's only sandwiches, but I don't have my dishes yet and flatware. Until that comes in and gets washed, we're doing finger foods. But, I promise you Quinn, as soon as we can have guests, you'll be our first invitation."

"I'll make sure you keep that promise."

She laughed, but her eyes met his and they shared a silent message. He wasn't sure what that message was. For his part, it was thank you. For hers, he wasn't sure. But, he liked that they could now do that.

He took a bite of the sandwich Grace had made. She'd bought hoagie buns and cold cuts. With lettuce, cucumbers, and tomatoes on top, it was delicious.

Grace took a deep breath. "I'm a bit nervous for tonight. I don't want to leave Chiefy here alone. We haven't been here long enough for her to feel comfortable alone. I don't want to leave her at the bungalow, because she's seen us move out and her things are here now. And, I'm afraid those bikers will do something and she'll get hurt."

Sid put his sandwich down and swallowed his food. "We can bring her with us. Keep her on the leash next to you. Your table will be close to the bar, away from the music so you can explain what the petition is about. She'll be able to lay in the sand, near you. And, if it gets to be too much for her, I'll park my truck close to you and she can sit in there with the window open where she can see you."

"Are you sure?"

"I'm sure."

Quinn nodded. "That's a great solution. I don't see anything wrong with it. She's well-behaved."

He saw Grace take a deep breath and exhale. "Okay. Thank you both."

He reached over and squeezed her shoulder in support. Her eyes stared into his and he felt the connection. They were connected in some special way. It felt good. His heart squeezed.

A knock on the door startled them all. Chiefy ran to the door and barked. Grace stood and moved toward the door.

He stood. "Grace. No. I'll get it. Then we'll set the cameras up, so we can see on our phones who's coming."

She stopped, her eyes watching his. He shrugged. "Just in case. Okay?"

She nodded and he kissed the top of her head as he moved to the door. First order of business, get a peephole.

He cracked the door open to find a delivery driver standing there, holding a box that looked heavy. "Hi."

The driver grinned. "Hey, there. I have a couple of packages for Grace Murphy."

"She's here. I'll take that one."

Taking the heavy package from the driver, he turned to see Quinn standing at the ready in case he was needed. They had each other's six. Always. He handed the box to Quinn, then followed the driver out to the truck for two more boxes.

He neared the house, and Quinn came out and took one of the boxes. As they neared the door he said to Quinn, "Can you install a peephole in the front door?"

"Can do."

"I appreciate it."

He set the boxes on the counter and watched Grace eagerly slice open the boxes with a utility knife. She chuckled. "It's like Christmas morning, except I know what's in here and I'm still excited."

He and Quinn chuckled. He glanced at Quinn, "Let's get the spare bed set up."

34

Grace finished dressing for the party. She wore a long flowy white skirt with a soft blue sleeveless blouse. Checking the mirror once more she took a deep breath and left the bedroom. Truth be told, she was tired. Sid was too. He'd fallen asleep on top of the bed while she was in the shower. When she came out of the shower and found him sleeping peacefully, she wanted to climb up next to him and sleep too. Instead, she sadly kissed his temple and rubbed his back. "You have to get ready for the party, sweetheart." She crooned.

His eyes opened slowly, a grin spread his lips and he reached out and pulled her tightly to him. "Sleep with me."

She giggled. "I'd love nothing more. But, I promised Jace we'd be there early to set up."

He sighed heavily. Kissing her ear softly he groaned. "I'm getting old Grace. Today damned near took its toll."

She giggled. "I can feel it too. Moving is not for the faint of heart. And, we had hardly anything to move. Until your things arrive from home."

"Yep. And, between now and then, we have a ton of things to do. First order of business, run the bikers out of town."

She laughed. "It sounds so easy when you say it like that."

Lying close together, his chuckle vibrated through her body. His lips kissed the back of her neck, then he sighed. "Okay. I'm jumping in the shower. I meant to join you in yours, but..."

She laughed. "I was hoping you would. We could christen the shower."

He rolled off the bed. "I love the way you think. We'll absolutely do that."

She watched her tired man slog his way to the shower. If they had more time, she'd absolutely join him.

On a deep breath, she rose and padded out to the kitchen. She pulled Chiefy's travel bowl from her little cupboard, and a little baggy of dog food in case she needed a snack. Chiefy laid on her bed in the kitchen, but she watched everything going on. She was a smart girl, she knew Grace was packing up for a little foray. Her tail thumped a couple of times.

Grace rummaged in the bedroom closet, promising herself she'd finish unpacking things tomorrow. Then they were going down to get Sid's things from his bungalow and get him moved into this house.

The shower shut off and she glanced at the clock on the stove. They had about thirty minutes to get down there. Her stomach quelled and she pressed her hand to her belly. Hopefully this would work. Hopefully, the bikers would get wind of what was happening and just leave town without issues. They had made themselves unwanted here. They likely did that everywhere they went.

Sid strutted down the hall toward her, a sexy smile on his face. He wore khaki shorts and a white button-down Hawaiian shirt. He looked handsome as ever, but tropical and warm too. She turned to face him as he reached her. She kissed his lips. "Hmm, you smell good."

He chuckled. "So do you. Should we skip tonight? I've gotten my second wind."

She laughed. "Oh, I think you'd get that wind knocked out of you by Jace if we skipped. After all he's done for us."

Sid groaned. "You're right." He kissed her again. This time it was soft and slow and sexy. Their tongues danced together, their bodies pressed tightly to each other. She loved the way they felt together. They fit together like puzzle pieces.

He squeezed her to him for the warmest hug she'd ever felt in her life. He meant it. She hugged him right back. His lips opened to say something, but he halted, swallowed, then nodded once. The realization that he was so touched he couldn't say anything floored her. It also made her eyes water. She inhaled deeply and sniffed lightly as her nose tingled.

She stepped back again, and let out the breath she'd taken in a whoosh. "Okay. That was deep."

He nodded. "I love you, Grace."

She stared into his eyes. This time it was more than the beautiful color that had her staring. She wanted to see his sincerity. It was there for her. He never looked away from her. He wasn't hiding as if he'd just said something he didn't mean.

"I love you too, Sid. I think from the first day."

He nodded. "The first day."

A chime sounded from their security cameras. Sid kissed her softly. He then sighed heavily and looked at his phone. When his eyes lifted to hers, his jaw tightened. "The bikers are at the bottom of the driveway."

She nodded. "Okay."

Sid nodded slowly as he looked at his phone. He heaved out a heavy sigh. "So, if they do something to the house after we leave, we'll have it on camera and they'll go to jail. That's one way to get them out of town. And, though we've both fallen in love with the house, the main thing is we'll all be out of the house if they get so bold."

She swallowed the huge lump that instantly formed in her throat. "Yeah."

"Grace. Nothing matters more than the safety of the three of us."

He wrapped his arm around her shoulders and pulled her tightly to his side. "Just the three of us." He restated.

"I know you're right. And, honestly that is all that matters. But, to think they may be so bold as to come up here and harm this gorgeous home, makes me incredibly sad."

He kissed her temple and squeezed once more. "Just as a precaution, do you have anything here you want to take with you? A special ring or memento from a parent or grandparent? Anything you want to keep close?"

Was it sad that she didn't have anything like that? It was sort of sad. "No. I don't have anything like that."

"Okay. So, the three of us will leave here together. We'll go down to the party and collect as many signatures as we can. And, if these assholes are bold enough to come up here, we'll have it on camera, and I'll call the police the instant they break the plane of the camera."

"Okay." She stood tall, inhaled and exhaled to bolster

her confidence, and get rid of the sadness that had crept in. Sid was right. It was all about the three of them.

She twisted and pulled the beach bag she'd filled with Chiefy's bowls and food, along with her petitions, a clipboard, and a handful of pens. She slung it over her shoulder and nodded at Sid. "Ready."

He nodded, but she saw him take a look around at the house as they left , and her heart hurt for him. For both of them. It was his dream too. They found this little dream that was beginning to come true and those assholes were trying to take it away from them. She was going to talk up that petition tonight and make those jerks leave this town.

35

Sid's stomach twisted as they drove down the driveway and the bikers were there. They now knew no one was home. The new house, their new home, now felt a bit like a sacrificial lamb to the slaughter. And, if they got wind of what the party was all about, desperation may drive them to do things they wouldn't normally do. Grace's little bungalows were also at risk and the Garage, his new place of business was as well.

He let out a long breath and tried to clear his head. Grace reached over and laid her hand on his arm. "I'm going to remain positive and put out positive energy."

He glanced her way briefly, then turned to the road. "Okay. I will too."

Chiefy licked his ear, then sniffed his ear, which tickled. He laughed and lifted his shoulder. Reaching back, he patted the side of her head and gave her a little squeeze. "You're a good girl, Chiefy."

He saw Grace smile from the corner of his eye and the pressure he felt in his chest lifted as he had all that mattered right here in his truck. Just like he'd told Grace earlier, all that mattered was the three of them in this truck.

He turned into the parking lot at the Sandbar and slowly drove his truck to the edge of the sand near the building, so Grace and Chiefy would be able to see each other, or if Chiefy needed a break and had to lay in the truck. Plus, it blocked Grace from the road should the bikers drive by. And they would. Especially when the music started.

He got out of the truck and hustled around to the passenger side. Helping Grace down he whispered near her ear, "I forgot to tell you how incredible you look."

She giggled. "Thank you." Then she tilted her head and looked up at him. Her smile was infectious, and he smiled in return.

"I can't wait to get home tonight. I've been thinking about you all day. We need to christen our new home. Maybe the Florida room first."

"It'll be hot and steamy out there. It's still eighty-six degrees outside and it's not supposed to cool down more than five more degrees tonight."

He shook his head once. "Oh, sweetheart, I look forward to hundreds of steamy nights with you."

The blue in her eyes deepened slightly as she laughed. "Steamy nights it is."

"Hey, you two, let's get you set up." Jace called as he exited the building.

Sid opened Chiefy's door and let her out, then reached in and grabbed Grace's beach bag with Chiefy's water bowl and food.

Grace took her bag as Jace arrived to greet them. He hugged his friend and was surprised when Jace hugged

Grace as well. Even Chiefy got a pat on the head and a 'Hello'.

"This is the table we have set up for you. I've got some signage for the front of the table. Theresa will be out here with it soon. Other than that, the servers will come along every so often to make sure you and Chiefy have enough water, and if you're hungry let them know."

"Okay."

Grace began unpacking the petitions she'd brought and the clipboard. She set pens on the table and Jace nodded to him.

"As soon as people start coming in, the servers will tell folks about the petition. You, Quinn, and I will circulate around the guests and tell them about it and encourage them to sign it. And, Hart & the Hurricanes will also announce often what the petition is for."

Sid's heart felt full as he listened to his friend's preparations for tonight. He'd thought of everything.

Sid's phone chimed and he frowned as he pulled it from his pocket. The bikers triggered the camera. He turned his phone to Jace and shook his head. "It doesn't look like they've gone up yet, but they're testing the cameras."

"Then let's send the cops there to show them the cameras work."

Sid nodded. He dialed 911 and held the phone to his ear. When the operator answered he told them quickly what was happening, and she said she'd have officers go up there and make sure everything was alright.

Sid heaved out a sigh of relief and before he'd hung up, the sirens could be heard. He turned and watched the road as the squad cars sped past. The town was small and the station not far away. He glanced at Grace and she blew him a kiss. They were in this together. That made his heart sing.

Quinn stepped out of the bar and strode toward him with a grin on his face. "Are those cops heading to your place?"

Sid grinned. "At least to the end of the driveway. The bikers are there and testing the cameras, I assume. So, we wanted them to know they work."

Quinn burst out laughing and clapped his hands together. "I love that."

Jace joined them after chatting with a few customers who were now talking to Grace.

"Okay, what we'll do tonight is mix and mingle. Chat with the guests, tell them about the petition and why it's so important. Get them to go over and chat with Grace. I just heard her explaining it to guests and she's killing it."

A man stepped from the bar and made his way to Jace.

"Hey there, Tony!" Jace shook his hand and clapped him on the back. "Sid Hoffman this is Tony Baluco. Quinn Kurtz- Tony Baluco. Tony manages Hart & the Hurricanes."

They shook hands and Tony grinned. "We'll announce often about the petition. Also, Jami Hart felt strongly about enough security, so he hired a private firm to cover the venue here and your garage Sid. Jace shared how this all started and none of us feel as though it's alright. We're here for you."

"I appreciate it. So does Grace. Thank you so much. I'll thank Jami also."

Tony laughed. "We appreciate it. I'll make sure you both meet the band. We're fired up and happy to be home for a while. We've been on the road touring."

The musicians and a couple of roadies began carrying

equipment to the outdoor stage and setting it all up. A couple women squealed when they saw who was playing tonight. That was his cue to get them to sign the petition.

"I'll chat later. Since those gals over there are excited about the band, I'm going to take advantage of that and tell them about the petition."

"Hello, I see you're excited about seeing Hart & the Hurricanes."

"We are. I didn't realize they were playing tonight."

"Are you residents of Blossom Springs?"

"I just moved here three weeks ago."

"Well, let me tell you why the band is here." Sid proceeded to tell the table about the petition, then wandered around and told another then another. Quinn and Jace were also milling about and he saw a line at the table near Grace. Chiefy laid on the sand behind the table, near Grace's chair and he smiled.

A man at a table waved him over. "You're the guy who got the Knucklehead running aren't you?"

Sid laughed. "One and the same."

"Nice job on that. Are you going to continue to fix it up?"

"I'm going to bring her back to her glory. It may take a while, but I'll get it finished."

"That's awesome. Coop is a great guy. He's found a good one in you."

"Thank you so much. I appreciate the compliment."

He spent the next few hours in much the same way. People recognized him as the guy fixing the Knucklehead. And he told them about the petition.

G race met so many people tonight. After three and a half hours, she had a short break and saw that she'd not only gotten her five hundred signatures, but she was now well over seven hundred. She couldn't wait to tell Sid. Chiefy whined a little and Grace bent down to pet her.

She opened the door to the truck, brushed Chiefy off with her hands, and Chiefy jumped inside. Grace rolled the window down so Chiefy could see her, but her tired pup was grateful to lay on a soft seat.

More folks approached the table and Grace started her spiel all over again. At this rate, she'd be saying it in her sleep.

She'd passed nervousness hours ago. And, now when people greeted her and asked her where she was from, she happily told them she lived here and she was fixing up her short-term rentals. A couple people said they had family coming into town and would look at her listing and rent it for them to stay in. This night turned out to be a boon not only for the petition, but for her little fledgling business too.

Sid drew closer and her tummy felt as though butterflies took flight.

He stepped behind the table and waited as she explained the petition one more time. After the folks left, Sid kissed her. "How are things going?"

"We now have seven hundred and sixty-five signatures." She chuckled. "We have enough and a few more just in case some of these aren't valid."

He hugged her close and whispered in her ear. "Damn I'm proud of you, but sweetheart, I'm beat."

She squeezed him tightly to her. "I'm tired too. But, revved about this petition."

"You should be. We did it."

"We did." She looked over at the band. "They're really good."

"They are. Jami is our neighbor. He lives in the house in front of the barn. The barn has been converted into a studio. Do you want to meet him?"

"I would."

"Okay. Let's pack this up and put it in the truck. How's our girl?"

"She's tired. She's sniffed the air until she has no more smell left I think. She laid down a while ago and that wasn't comfortable anymore, so I put her in the truck. I tried brushing the sand off her, but if I didn't get it all, I'll clean your truck tomorrow."

He chuckled. "Don't fret over it. It's all good."

She packed up her petitions. Then grabbed Chiefy's water bowl and dumped out the water that was left. Using a napkin, she dried it out then tucked that in her bag.

Sid grabbed all the pens off the table and dropped

them in her bag, then took it from her and set it in the truck. He opened the back door and petted Chiefy, then closed the door and took her hand. They skirted the tables, chairs, and the dancers and made it to the side of the stage just as the band announced their break. She watched the band members as they played. They all looked like they were having fun. That said so much about them all. They had talent and managed to find work they loved to boot.

As soon as the band stopped for their break, Jami met them at the side of the stage. Sid smiled as he looked at her. "Jami, I'd like you to meet my girl, Grace Murphy. Grace, Jami Hart."

Jami shook her hand and smiled. "Nice to meet you, neighbor."

Grace giggled. Which, for a woman her age seemed odd. But, Jami Hart was handsome and talented and she saw all the women swooning as they listened to his sultry voice croon love songs and songs of woe. "Nice to meet you too."

Jami grinned. "So, how did we do? Did you get the signatures you needed?"

"We did and then some. Thank you so very much for playing tonight and helping us with this. I don't know how I'll ever be able to thank you."

"Getting those bikers out of town is how you'll thank me. I love this little town. It's my sanctuary. I don't want it ruined."

Grace nodded. "Thank you just the same. We're doing what we can."

She turned to Sid who stood smiling and watching her. Tony Baluco came over and said hello. He introduced them to backup singer, Livia, Sean West the bass player,

Axel Peters the drummer, and Mads Nolan backup singer. She'd never met an entire band and not one of this caliber. She was smitten and excited. The band floated off to get something to drink and chill for a few moments and Sid took her hand and walked with her to the water. Lights from the tiki bar reflected beautifully on the waves as they lapped the sand on the shore. She took her sandals off and carried them in her left hand as Sid held her right hand. They walked slowly along the water's edge, both of them enjoying this bit of quiet peacefulness.

Sid stopped and pulled her into his arms and kissed her softly. He rested his forehead against hers, his voice gruff when he softly said, "I love you, Grace. I've wanted to shout it out all night."

She chuckled. "I love you too, Sid. We love you, Chiefy and I."

He chuckled and kissed her softly once more. "Let's go home and seal the deal, shall we? I want to make love to you tonight in our new home."

37

hiefy, usually in the backseat looking out the windshield, licking his ear or Grace's cheek, or generally looking out the window, slept all the way home. Which, granted wasn't that far, but she didn't stir. There were no bikers in sight on the road, which made them both smile. Turning up the driveway, he could see this being his future. Grace and Chiefy in the truck with him, driving up their scenic driveway, eager to end the evening together in their beautiful home.

He pulled to a stop at the top of the driveway, next to Grace's car. She opened her door and Sid's head whipped around to look at her. "I love opening your door for you."

Her smile was perfect, but tired. "I love that you do. But, I thought you were tired."

"Honey, I'm tired, you're tired. Even Chiefy's tired. But, that doesn't mean we get lazy about the little things I do to show you I love you. Once couples get lazy, things begin to fade. Let's not fade away."

Her throat moved as she swallowed, their eyes locked

on each other's for some time. She took a deep breath. "Thank you."

He nodded once and jumped from the truck. Opening Grace's door, he held his hand out to her, kissed her fingers when she placed them in his hand, and steadied her as she stepped down to the ground. Chiefy stood in the backseat, her panting now steaming up the windows.

He opened the back door as Grace gathered her bag and purse, Chiefy jumped down, sniffed a bit and peed. Then the three of them walked to the house together.

Inside, Grace checked Chiefy's dishes for food and water. Chiefy checked them too. Sid locked the doors, then watched in wonder at the turn in his life in such a short amount of time. Grace joined him at the beginning of the hallway and hand in hand they walked to the bedroom.

Inside the bedroom, Chiefy found her bed and turned about five circles before settling in. He shrugged his clothes off as did Grace and they slid into their big bed, facing the windows, with the view of the water below.

Grace rolled over and kissed his lips. Softly, gently, her tongue slipped into his mouth and slid along his tongue. His hands found her ass, and pulled her up. Her soft, full breasts against his chest felt like heaven, and his cock twitched.

Grace straddled him, their lips still seeking, searching, molding to the others. She began to rock against his cock, and his breathing became short stutters of air coming in and leaving. His heartbeat increased to a rapid tempo, much like Hart & the Hurricane's had played tonight, the music still ringing in his ears. When Grace sat up, the moonlight played across her body in a hypnotic dance, the waves of the water casting shadows and lights on her skin. He reached forward and filled his hands with her breasts, squeezing lightly, enjoying the feel of her soft warm flesh against his work-roughened hands. Her lips turned up in a smile, her hair fell about her shoulders in soft dark waves. She was a siren calling him to do unspeakable things to her and he was only happy to oblige.

He slid his hands down to her belly. It was soft and slightly rounded. It was the first time she'd allowed him to fully see her body. He wasn't disappointed. She was beautiful.

She rose up slightly and fit the head of his cock to her entrance, pushing down slightly so the head was covered in her moisture. She grinned a sassy grin, splayed her hands over his chest, and slowly lowered herself onto his cock. It was the sexiest thing he had ever in his entire life seen and felt. It was exquisite.

He heard a groan, believed it came from him, but honestly, all he cared about right now was Grace. She lifted and lowered herself over and over, each time those gorgeous breasts bounced and moved and he didn't know if he wanted to watch her face, her breasts, or where they were joined together. In the end, he watched her breasts dance to and fro as she lifted and lowered. They were perfect.

Her movements grew faster, their skin heated and she had an ethereal glow. Incredible.

He placed his hands on her hips and helped her to reach her release, the moans that escaped from her were hypnotic and rhythmic and musical.

She panted harder, "Sid." She huffed out. He smiled as he looked into her eyes. "Let it go, baby."

She moved a few more times, faster and faster, until

she cried out his name once more as her body jerked. She fell onto his chest and he wrapped her in his arms. Allowing her a moment, his body sought its own release, and he lifted his hips and held hers in place as he managed to pump into her a few times and let his orgasm rage out of him. He jerked and moved until the last of his seed had spilled, then he wrapped his arms tightly around her body and held her close. They fell asleep just like that and he'd never forget that night for as long as he lived. He knew that immediately. It was simply perfection.

Grace put her right hand over her tummy and inhaled deeply.

Sid squeezed her left hand, "Ready?"

She let the air in her lungs whoosh out and nodded. "Yeah."

Sid hustled around the truck to open her door. He patted Chiefy on the head and held her hand as they walked together into the city hall building to turn in her petition and signatures.

She sent out a silent prayer that she'd done everything correctly so everything everyone did wasn't lost. Navigating the halls, they found the door to the clerk's office. Her hands shook slightly as she pulled the papers from her bag. The clerk came to the front desk and smiled.

"How can I help y'all?"

"Hi. I have a signed petition for a special session of the city council to be called, and an emergency order on the nuisance and destruction the bikers have been causing in town."

"Oh, I heard about that. My daughter and two of her

friends went last night to hear Jami Hart. She's been a fan of his for a long time. Three of the gals here went last night too."

"That's great. It was my first time hearing Hart & the Hurricanes. I loved their music."

"Me too. He's a nice young man too."

Grace stifled a giggle. Jami Hart was easily her age, which was fifty. But, the clerk standing in front of her could have been nearing seventy.

"Yes, he is."

The clerk looked through the papers. "I see you came in right as we opened this morning, you must feel strongly about this petition." Grace only nodded. She clicked on the computer a few times, typed something out, waited for a long time, at least it felt like it.

She then asked, "What's your name sweetheart?"

"Grace. Grace Murphy."

"Okay." She tapped a few times. "And your name, sugar?" She asked Sid.

He grinned. "Sid Hoffman."

"Oh, you're the man making things happen here in town aren't you. I hear you bought the Garage from Coop. And the house on the bluff too."

Sid nodded. "That's me."

"Nice. Coop should have retired years ago. That old man should be taking his wife on vacation instead of going to work every day. They have all the money they'll ever need. Know what I mean?"

Sid chuckled. "I do. Coop's a man with a mind of his own. He'll do what he'll do, when he's ready."

The clerk shrugged one shoulder. "Just doesn't seem fair to Fanny is all."

Neither she nor Sid responded and the clerk tapped

away on her computer. "Looks like the only night we can squeeze in a special session is tonight." She tapped a couple of times and the printer whirred as papers popped out. "Six o'clock right here in city hall. You need to be here when your petition is discussed."

"We'll be here." Grace responded. Her voice sounded slightly shaky, but excitement coursed through her. The paperwork went through.

The clerk handed her the papers. "These signatures will be verified and if there aren't enough valid signatures, your petition won't be heard. I've got to let you know that."

"Okay."

The excitement of a moment ago subsided and a gnawing fear replaced it. Sid put his arm around her shoulders and squeezed. "It's all good, Grace. We've got this. And, if not, we did the best we could."

"Yeah." They walked out of the city hall building and jumped in the truck.

"I'll drop you at your house, then head to the Garage. Will you be alright there alone today?"

"Yes. I'll have Chiefy and my car isn't sitting outside so the bikers won't know I'm in there."

"They will when you have to let Chiefy out."

"I think I'll only go out the back door and stay back there. Until you come to get us to go to the beach this evening, we'll be hidden. Plus, they'll likely be watching the first house, not realizing I own the one next door and that's where we'll be."

"Okay. Keep your phone on you and if anything, even the slightest thing scares you, give me a call."

She chuckled. "I will."

"Why do you find that funny?"

She turned her head to look at him. "I've never had

anyone so protective of me. I'll be honest, it's...nice, but I'm not used to it."

He reached over and took her hand. "I don't want anything to happen to you."

"Then, we'll stay hidden if I see a biker, and I'll call you if anything scares me."

"Perfect."

He turned down Sunset Beach Road and they both heaved out a sigh of relief. No bikers.

He glanced at her and winked, she couldn't help but giggle, just a bit. She'd done everything to the best of her ability, and that had finally sunk in. Now, she just felt...happy.

Sid pulled into the driveway and she leaned over and kissed his lips. "If you want I can leave my truck here in case you need to get out of here or get something. I can cut across the footpath."

"I think we'll be fine. Since it's the first day in this place, I'll be cleaning the walls to paint them, and making a plan for the rest."

She saw his Adam's apple bob. "Sid?"

He looked into her eyes. "Grace."

"We'll be fine. Look, they may have lost interest in us. They aren't here this morning. Maybe they found out what last night's party was about and they've decided to leave on their own terms."

"I won't let my guard down until I know they're gone."

Grace shifted in her seat slightly. "Where are they staying?"

"I asked around and apparently they're in the campground north of town. It sounds like they've gotten into a bit of trouble there though and were threatened with eviction."

"Oh, my gosh. Troublemakers no matter where they go."

"Yep."

She leaned over the console and kissed his lips. "See you at lunch today?"

"Yes. What can I bring you?"

"I wouldn't mine the sriracha tacos."

He chuckled. "You got it."

39

S id drove to the garage with a light heart. He and Grace worked together along with his friends to set the wheels in motion to save their new little town.

Parking his truck alongside the garage, Coop was already there working on a car. Sid entered, "Good morning."

"Morning, Sid. How was the party last night?"

"It was good. We got all the signatures we needed. We've already taken them to city hall and they've set the meeting for tonight."

"That's wonderful news. I've been hearing all morning what a nice time it was. That Jami Hart is really making a name for himself."

Sid chuckled. "Oh, Lordy, the women were swooning last night."

Coop shook his old head and chuckled. "I've heard."

Coop pulled the shop rag from the pocket of his bib overalls and wiped his hands. "So, my attorney has the paperwork drawn up. I have it here for you in the office.

Anytime you want to sign on the dotted line, the old Garage is yours."

A thrill ran down Sid's spine. His heartbeat sped up and his throat dried. He was doing this. "I'm ready any day you are Coop. I have the money in the bank in town and we can go there together to get it or I can have it deposited to your account. Whatever you like."

Faded blue eyes stared into his and he saw the emotions whirling in Coop. The old man sniffed. He nodded his head slowly. "Will I be able to stop in and work on something from time to time?"

Sid chuckled. "I'd love for you to stop in and help me with my work. Plus, the company is always nice."

"That it is. I've enjoyed spending time with you these past weeks. You're a good man, Sid."

Sid grinned and his eyes watered slightly. "You're a good man too, Coop."

"Ehh, I've tried to be. I don't have a lot of patience. I've entered the time in my life where...what do the kids say? I don't have any more fucks to give. Yeah, that's it. I won't be badgered or bullied. I just want to come to work, not worry about things, and make broken vehicles whole again."

Sid grinned at the old man's honesty. "I'm right there with you Coop. I promise you I'll run an honest garage. There'll be no bullshit here. Except that of friends stopping in to shoot it. I'm hardworking, and I'll treat this business you've built with respect."

"I know you will, Sid. That's why I picked you."

Sid chuckled.

The sound of a motorcycle caused his back to grow rigid and he fought turning around to look, but he heard two bikes pull into the lot and stop and he knew he had to deal with it. His eyes rested on Coop's for a moment, and the old man nodded. "I'll have my finger on the phone to call the police."

Sid nodded and turned to address the bikers.

He didn't have the chance to say anything before they started talking. "We have a bike that needs fixin'."

Sid shook his head, he pulled his body up straight, his shoulders wide, his stance shoulder width apart. Just like in the military. "I've already told you guys I'm not working on your bikes."

"This is a garage, isn't it?"

"It is."

"Maybe we need to speak to the owner."

"You are."

The biker leaned over to look into the garage at Coop. "I thought he was the owner."

"He was. I am now."

The two bikers looked at each other. Sid could almost see them seething and trying to figure out how to get their way without having the police called on them.

The taller of the two took a small step toward Sid. "We always get our way. People don't turn us down or things happen to them."

He chose not to respond. Instead he stared at them with the deadest stare he could muster. Straight ahead, no emotion.

The shorter biker laughed. "Things happen to their women too. Maybe we need to go on over and teach that woman of his what a real man is like in the sack."

Anger slithered through Sid hotter and meaner than any he'd ever felt in his life. These two fuckers wouldn't lay a hand on Grace. Not while he was alive. He felt his cheeks heat and the fire that was lit in his belly had him already sweating, despite this morning's temperature being a nice seventy-four.

The two bikers laughed at their antics. They thought they were funny. They also thought they were scaring him. What scared him were the deadly thoughts running through his mind right now. Never had he been so angry to think of killing someone with his bare hands.

The tall biker cocked his hip out. "What'll it be grease monkey. Fix our bike or we go fuck your woman." He gyrated his hips to emphasize his intention.

Sid took a deep breath, mostly to get his emotions reined in enough to speak clearly and succinctly. "You two will do what you'll do whether I fix your bike or not. You're not honest folks so I have no reason to believe you'll do the right thing even if I do fix your bike. But, I'm telling you right now, I will not now, and not ever, be your mechanic. And..." He paused for effect. "If you touch one hair on my girl's head, I'll murder you both where you stand, and happily go to jail for it just to see your blank stares as the life flows out of you."

The shorter biker's smile melted away faster than an ice cream cone on a ninety-degree day. He cocked his head slightly. "That right? You're threatening us?"

"You just threatened me and my girl."

"But, we mean our threats. I don't think you have the balls to follow through on yours."

He felt the slow, evil smile crease his lips. He knew it was evil by the looks on the bikers' faces. He then took a step toward them and both of them straightened their posture. "Get out."

They stared for a long time, then the sound of sirens coming closer had them looking at each other. The tall one jerked his head toward the bikes. They both got on their motorcycles and started them up. Sid didn't move a muscle. He stared at them until they backed their bikes out of the driveway and took off down the street.

A squad car pulled into the parking lot and Sid stepped toward it. He leaned down and spoke to Officer Isak Voss, whom he'd met last night. "Please go down and check on Grace. They've threatened to do unspeakable things to her. I'll be here to make a statement after you check on her."

"Will do, Sid."

The police car sped away and he pulled his phone out to call Grace. They were going to get these fuckers out of this town.

Grace dressed for the night in a pair of white capri pants and a soft yellow blouse. She'd been as nervous as a cat in a room of rocking chairs all afternoon after Sid called and the police stopped. She opted to come home when Sid suggested it. At least here they had cameras and the police were able to patch into their security system to be alerted when someone breached the cameras. They didn't do that often, but they did do it when necessary, such as now. Also, the threat of bodily harm from the bikers, mixed with the acts of violence they'd already demonstrated helped their cause.

She took a deep breath and moved toward the kitchen. Sid was in the shower and would want something to eat before they went to the council meeting.

She fed Chiefy, then looked into the refrigerator for something to eat.

"What are you looking for in there that's taking so long?"

She whirled around, startled at his voice. "Oh, you scared me."

He shook his head. "Honey, I'm sorry for that. I surely didn't mean to scare you."

"It's just..." She motioned around with her hands. "Today."

He pulled her close. "I know. Let's go to town and attend our meeting. Let's do what we can to get them to leave our town."

"What if they don't leave?"

"I don't know. Do you know how to use a gun?"

"It's been years. But, I was trained in the Army and then after, I used to practice with girlfriends. We had a shooting club back home."

"Okay. Do you have a gun?"

"Not anymore."

He nodded. He sat at one of the stools at the center bar. "We'll remedy that tomorrow. Also, tomorrow, I'm officially buying the Garage. And, I need a new sign made. I think I want a logo and everything."

"Oh, honey, that's awesome." She hugged him close and closed her eyes as she let his love seep in.

"Thanks. It's all because of you. You've given me my life back. You've given me love. You've given me my confidence."

"Oh, honey. You had all of that in you. If I helped to bring it out of you, I'm so very happy. You deserve everything good in life."

"I have it now."

She squeezed him again, and his arms tightened around her waist. They stood like that for some time, each of them needing the other.

"I was going to make you something to eat."

He pulled away slightly. "I'm sure you don't feel like making me something to eat with the council meeting pending. And, to be honest, I'm not sure I could eat. So, how about we go down to the meeting, then we'll stop at the Sandbar afterwards and eat."

"That sounds good." She stepped back and looked into his eyes. "I can't leave Chiefy here, Sid. If they come here to do something to the house, she'll be injured. I can't..."

Her voice cracked and she didn't say anything further. He nodded. "We'll take Chiefy with us. I think they'll allow her in the building as my emotional support dog. She's well-behaved and she'll be with us and safe."

"I'd appreciate that."

He chuckled. "Honey, we're a family now. I feel that in my heart. You and Chiefy are my family and I'm yours."

She teared up. It was fast and hot and the emotion hit her right in her heart. She swallowed and nodded. "We're your family and you are ours."

"Right."

A tear fell and she dabbed it away and took a deep breath, then blew it out. "Okay. I think I'm ready."

Sid chuckled and it sounded so good. "Me too. Let's go get those bikers."

She chuckled. "Let's go get 'em."

Chiefy jumped up and pranced around as if she knew what was going on. Grace pulled her leash from the hook by the door, Sid pulled her portable water dish from the cupboard and a bottle of water for her.

They strutted to the truck together. She and Sid, hand in hand, Chiefy on the leash beside her.

Sid turned into the city hall building and they were both shocked. The lot was nearly full. People turned out for the meeting.

She perused all the vehicles and her mouth dropped open. "Wow."

Sid chuckled. Even Coop had driven over tonight.

They entered the building, Chiefy in tow. The clerk looked over the counter at Chiefy, then up to each of them. "Emotional support?"

Grace smiled. "Yes." She was in all aspects. She may not have that exact label or the vest, but she was surely her support and had been for a number of years. Then, by choice, she became Sid's support. So, she was surely that.

"Come on back."

They followed the clerk through a set of doors where a large room was filled with the townspeople. The far wall, where the council sat, was a beautiful built-in half-circle desk made of oak, and behind it eight chairs and microphones.

Folks nodded when they saw them, many smiled. Grace recognized so many of them from last night. It was amazing. There weren't any seats available, they likely didn't have meetings with this kind of turnout very often. So, Sid steered them over to the far corner where they stood.

Soon a door behind the council desk opened, and eight people emerged, one of them the clerk.

The man in the middle, spoke into his microphone. "Good evening. I'm Roark Dinsmore, President of the Blossom Springs City Council. Tonight's meeting is a special meeting requesting an emergency order regarding the rash of property damage, citizen threats, and general mayhem caused by a certain group of bikers that have come to rest in Blossom Springs. The petition was brought by Grace Murphy. Ms. Murphy are you present?"

"Yes." She yelled from the back of the room.

"Please come forward and explain your petition."

She glanced at Sid, he winked and whispered, "You've got this." She handed him Chiefy's leash and made her way up the side aisle to the front of the council where a podium and microphone stood.

"Ms. Murphy. Please explain your petition so the council members and townspeople present can hear you."

"Yes sir." She took a deep breath and as succinctly as she could, she explained the situations as they happened to her. She finished by adding. "I know many others in this room have also experienced issues with the bikers. My..." She hesitated. Was Sid her boyfriend. It seemed silly to call him her boyfriend, they were of a certain age. Partner, she could say that. "My partner and I have both recently moved to Blossom Springs. We've both found a beautiful little town and have met the most wonderful people here. We're both starting businesses, and..." She turned and looked at Sid. "We've found each other."

Sid smiled and nodded at her and she turned back to the council. "We don't want these bikers, who have no ties here, no commitments here, to come in and wreck this beautiful little paradise. I urge you to give police the authority to arrest those bikers every time they cause damage. Personally, I'd love for them to be run out of town. But, mostly, we all have the right to feel safe in our homes, something Sid and I haven't managed to do since they began targeting his garage. We shouldn't have to worry that we'll show up at our businesses only to find they've been vandalized. Let's bring the peace and tranquility back to Blossom Springs."

The audience clapped and cheered, and her cheeks burned. She'd never presented to a city council before. And, she'd never had such a large audience before.

"Thank you, Ms. Murphy. The council will now hear from the townspeople."

One by one their friends, neighbors, and fellow towns-people stood before the council and shared their experiences with the bikers. In all, they were there for close to two hours. She and Sid stood quietly in the back, though her feet were sore and tired and her back was beginning to ache, she waited and clapped as each person told their sad tale.

The council excused themselves to deliberate privately, while the folks in the room took the opportunity to chat with each other. Sid took her hand and pulled her toward Coop. They knelt down alongside him, and his old, wrinkled hand patted Chiefy. "You did a good job, Grace."

"Thank you, Coop."

"Did your man here tell you he's officially the owner of the Garage tomorrow?"

She smiled at him. "He sure did. You still have some time to back out."

Coop laughed. "No, thank you. I've had my time in the Garage, it's Sid's turn."

He patted Sid on the shoulder and grinned ear to ear.

The council reentered the room and the crowd quieted down.

She laid her hand over her stomach as it quelled. The clerk glanced her way and, was that a grin on her face? Grace would have sworn she grinned at her.

"The council meeting will come to order," Roark Dinsmore barked.

The crowd silenced and Roark again leaned forward into the microphone.

"The council has discussed the stories we've heard

tonight. Ms. Murphy, your petition was required to have five hundred signatures. You brought in seven hundred and seventy-two. Of those, seventy-eight were erroneous and unable to be verified as citizens on the voting rolls of Blossom Springs. That still left you with six hundred and ninety-four valid signatures. Congratulations on managing this in such a short amount of time."

She smiled. "I had plenty of help from friends."

"I've heard. You have some powerful friends Ms. Murphy. Remind me to get you on my re-election campaign."

The crowd laughed and she did too. It felt good to laugh.

"The council voted and unanimously approved the emergency order. It will not run the bikers out of town, so to speak. But, we'll make it irritating for them to live here. Police will immediately be instructed to arrest the bikers involved in any theft, vandalism, stalking, and threat of bodily harm. We'll either have them all in jail or they'll get tired of being hauled in. In addition, the fines for such violations will be doubled until the bikers leave town. So as not to show any profiling and open ourselves up to that criticism, the fines are doubled right now for everyone committing any crime, harassment, theft, vandalism, and/or stalking." He tapped the gavel to the block. "Meeting adjourned."

The council stood up to leave and the room erupted in cheers and applause. Sid grabbed her and hugged her tightly. He kissed her lips. "Congratulations, sweetheart. You did it."

"With your help and Jace's and Quinn's and Jami's."

"You were the driving force."

People came up to congratulate her and thank her for

a job well-done and she met even more people than she had last night it seemed.

As people filtered out of the room, Sid took her hand and Chiefy's leash and led her to the door. "Let's go home and celebrate."

41

Sid walked out of the bank, a smile on his face and Grace at his side. Their hands were clasped tightly together and he'd never felt higher. He glanced down at her and saw her smiling face looking up at him.

"You own a business, Sid."

He chuckled as he had much of the morning. It all seemed so surreal. "I know. It doesn't seem real. All these years I felt like I was searching but not knowing what I was searching for. All these years, I felt like I didn't belong or I was doing something wrong but I didn't know why. It took coming here and finding you and Coop and the Garage to find where I was supposed to be. I know that sounds weird, but I don't have the words to describe it."

She rested her head on his shoulder. "I understand this, believe it or not. I understand it. It feels like you aren't a complete person and you're slogging along doing what you feel like you're supposed to do, but even that doesn't feel right."

"Yes." He shook his head. "Grace, you get me."

She laughed and the sound of it sent a thrill through him. "I do. I think you get me too. It's wonderful."

"It is." He helped her into his truck, then sauntered around to the driver's side. When he slid in, he glanced at her beautiful face and grinned. "I'd like to have a grand opening. Maybe a party or something."

"Oh, that's a great idea. I'll help you with that. Should we do it this weekend?"

"Absolutely. I'd like to get it over with so I can begin business in earnest."

Grace laughed. "Okay. Let me work on some things and plan for a party on Saturday. You just need to get the Garage organized so you can showcase it positively and let folks know you're in business."

He chuckled. "I'll get things organized. I wanted to do that anyway, so I have some bearing on what's here and what, if anything I'll need moving forward."

She smiled. Her hair blew slightly in the breeze, her lips had a shine on them, and her smile was breathtaking. His heart thumped firmly in his chest and he thought how many times in the last few weeks she'd made his heart pound and sing. At this time in his life, he hated to let a minute pass him by and yet, he didn't want to be rash either. His head had been spinning since he met Grace, and to be honest, he loved the way she made him feel.

He secured her into the truck then jumped in himself. They drove to her second bungalow. "If you feel scared in any way Grace, call me."

"I will. We all know now the police can arrest them. I feel better just knowing that."

"But, don't let that be a false security Grace. They can get to you faster than you can call if you let your guard down."

She smiled at him. Her smile was like the sun rose high. "I know. I won't let my guard down. I still have to protect Chiefy, even though she thinks she's protecting me."

"Right." He chuckled. He helped her out of the truck, then helped Chiefy down while Grace unlocked the door to the second bungalow. They'd swept up the dead bugs when they brought all the tools and paint over.

Chiefy ran into the bungalow and straight to the kitchen where her dishes were. She seemed to be doing a check. Sid did the same, checking to make sure no one hid inside and it was safe to leave them here. He locked the back door. He hugged Grace to him, kissed the top of her head and held her close for a while before pulling back.

"Okay. I've gotta go. I have a business to run."

She chuckled and slapped his butt. "Get going old man."

"Ouch."

"I didn't slap you that hard."

He grinned. "I meant the old man part. Ouch."

She laughed. He winked at her, turned the lock on the door on his way out, and felt like he was on cloud nine as he sauntered to his truck.

A few moments later he was pulling into his parking area. He sat in his truck a moment, staring at the Garage, trying to make his brain believe this had actually happened. Quinn's truck pulled in behind his and he laughed.

They met in the middle and he hugged his friend tightly. He both received and gave big thumps on the back.

He turned, as did Quinn, and both men stared at the Garage.

Quinn asked, "When are you getting a new sign?"

"As soon as I can. Do you know a good place to get one?"

"Yeah. I'll text you the information."

"Grace is planning a party on Saturday for a grand opening. I hope you and Jared will join us."

"I wouldn't miss it for the world. I've been on cloud nine since I heard you were buying this place. Both of my best friends here in the same town with me is like a dream. Other than the military, we've never lived in the same town together."

Sid thought for a moment. "You're right."

Quinn slapped him on the back once more. "I just wanted to come and wish you a happy first day at your place. If you need anything, holler. If those fuckers give you grief, get in touch with me. I've always got your six."

"Thanks, Quinn. I've got yours."

He'd always be there for his friends. They'd been through the shit together. They'd seen things most people never see. They had a bond that couldn't be broken.

Quinn gently punched him in the arm. "Gotta run buddy, but I'm never far away."

"Boy, don't I know that," Sid teased. Quinn laughed as he strode to his truck and Sid's heart felt light.

Coop pulled into the parking lot and got out of his truck. He shuffled toward Sid and chuckled. "You aren't going to get any work done staring at the place."

Sid laughed and shook his head. "As usual, you're right."

He unlocked the door for the first time as the owner. His fingers shook slightly as he realized it was all his now. And he and Coop started turning lights on and opening garage doors and getting ready for business.

Grace looked at the design on her computer. Did she love it? Yes, she did. Would Sid love it? She sure hoped so. The designer did such a great job with it. But, purples and teals and a heart in the middle might not be what Sid had in mind for his logo. She'd find out on Saturday.

They'd decided to grill burgers outside at the Garage on Saturday. Yesterday she called the grocery store to order everything. She'd pick it all up Saturday morning.

Her computer chimed the incoming email and the subject line excited her. "You have a booking".

Eagerly opening the email she squealed in delight. She had her first booking for her little bungalow for a whole week. She read through the reservation, saw they'd paid the required deposit to hold it, and they'd left a comment at the bottom asking if there were blow dryers and a coffee maker in the home.

Quickly replying, "You should find everything you need in the bungalow. Blow dryers in both bathrooms, coffee maker, toaster, dishes and pots & pans in the kitchen and basic utensils. I'm looking forward to your stay."

Her heart beat erratically and she jumped up from her chair and moved around the house to burn off some of her excitement. She'd work extra hard this week to get the second bungalow finished. She was finally on her way. Living with Sid had certainly eased some of the financial burden as far as she and Chiefy were concerned. Plus, she loved him. She enjoyed their time together. She once again ran her hand over the gleaming cool granite counter tops here in the house and smiled. She lived in a house like this and it was surreal.

Moving to the bedroom, she stepped in as Sid was pulling a t-shirt over his head. His head poked through the shirt and he grinned. "Are you watching me get dressed?"

"Yes."

Chiefy trotted into the room and looked up at him. "I'm going to start charging admission soon."

Grace laughed. "What will that cost me? I'll have to save up."

"I'll think of something." He scooped her off her feet and swung her around. As he set her feet back on the ground, he kissed her just like she liked it. Soft. Slow. Wet. It was perfect.

He swatted her butt lightly, and she giggled. "You ready for breakfast?"

"Yes." He patted Chiefy on the head, nuzzled with her which prompted her to flop on the floor and show him her belly. Sid laughed and obliged her belly rub and Grace watched happily.

"I got my first rental guests."

He chuckled. "That's awesome. When is your reservation for?"

"Next month."

"There you go, Grace. It's the start and what you've been waiting for. Congratulations. Wanna celebrate tonight?"

"What did you have in mind?"

"I thought we could sit in the Florida room with a couple glasses of wine and chat."

She smiled. "I'd love that."

She pulled eggs from the refrigerator and a pan from the cupboard. "Scrambled or fried today?"

"Scrambled sounds good."

"Coming right up."

Sid peeled an orange while she beat the eggs in a bowl. They'd fallen into a sweet routine this past week and she felt happier than she'd ever felt in her life. There had been great moments in her life, but she didn't remember them bringing her this much joy. But, it wasn't just joy, it was peace.

Sid set plates on the table and poured them each a cup of coffee. As they sat at the table, Sid scooped scrambled eggs from the pan and said, "The bikers tried breaking into the grocery store last night. Two of them are in jail this morning."

"How did you hear that?"

"Quinn."

"I've wondered about them. They've been rather quiet this week."

"Yeah. When they're quiet, I worry they're plotting."

"I agree. It's almost as if it's scarier when they're quiet."

"Yep."

They finished breakfast and cleaned up. She grabbed

Chiefy's leash and clipped it on her collar. She kissed Sid's lips and hugged him close. "I love you. Have a great day."

He chuckled. "I love you. I'll be around this afternoon to help you with the cabinets."

"I appreciate it. Thank you."

She got Chiefy into her car and Sid jumped into his truck. He waited for her to start her car and proceed down the driveway.

She pulled into the driveway of her bungalow and Sid tooted twice as he continued on. She and Chiefy entered the house, she locked the doors and called the person Quinn had told her about to create a new sign for Sid's garage. It was her grand opening gift to him. She couldn't wait to see his face when he saw it. The risk of having the logo designed without his input was her only concern. She still wondered if she should run the design past him, but keep the sign a secret.

She shook her head and shook off the negative feelings. She hated keeping a secret from him. Before beginning to paint, she made a couple of phone calls to prepare for Saturday. Then she'd get some work done, so she could get this little bungalow on the market too.

S id wheeled the grill out of the garage and started it up. As it warmed, he helped Grace with the folding tables.

"What do you think we should do with the tables, line them up?" he asked.

Grace shook her head. "I think we set them up in the driveway and parking area so it looks full, but is still easy to navigate. We can do them in rows of three with space between."

"Great idea."

He set the tables up, Grace put plastic tablecloths on each table.

He began lining up the hamburgers on the grill and the smell began filtering out, filling the air with the most delicious aroma. His stomach growled, despite having just eaten breakfast.

Quinn pulled up and parked on the street. "Put me to work," he called out.

Sid laughed. "You can either take over here at the grill or help Grace set up the tables."

Quinn shrugged. "Since you've got that smelling fantastic, I'll set up tables for Grace." He set up a few tables, "What's with the sign?"

Sid glanced up at the sign placed high on the garage, with a cover over it. "It's Grace's grand opening present to me."

"Have you seen it?"

"Nope. She refused to show me and said she wanted it to be a surprise. And, before you ask, no I didn't snoop. I wanted it to be a surprise too."

Jace came next, "What can I do?"

"How about hauling the box of buns sitting on the checkout counter out for Grace? She's setting up the food table." He nodded toward Grace, who happily set out paper plates, plastic forks, napkins, miniature bags of chips, and more. He'd asked that this be a simple, down-home-type event, to celebrate his purchase of the Garage, and let the town know he was the new owner. But, in truth, very little would change here at the Garage.

People began to filter into the garage, Quinn's workers all came for lunch. They worked Saturdays when they had jobs to do, but Quinn told them to come on over and grab a bite to eat.

Sid shook more hands than he ever had. Between today and the petition signing party last week, he felt he must have met everyone who lived here. Grace was also hostessing, making sure everyone had a water because it was incredibly hot outside.

All in all, his little grand opening seemed to be a success. Grace made her way to him. He stopped and watched her draw near. The smile on her face was one he always wanted to see. She was radiant.

She stopped before him. "Want to see your new sign?"

"I do."

She inhaled deeply. "Sid. I had a logo designed. I want you to know if you don't like it, we can redo it. I went with my gut on this. It doesn't look like your typical garage logo. But, it truly speaks to your vision of Miracle Garage. At least I think so."

She turned him around so he faced the garage and more importantly, the sign above it.

Grace nodded to Quinn's workers, who each held a rope in their hands to tug the cover off the sign. They each tugged and the cloth covering the sign floated down to the ground around them.

He stood staring at a purple and teal sign with starbursts around it. Two wrenches crossed the starbursts and the outline of a heart stood in the center. Miracle Garage was in white letters. He stood staring at it. It was official.

Grace stood silently beside him. He put his arm around her shoulders. They stared at it together, people behind them clapped their hands. "It's beautiful, Grace."

She turned in his arms and wrapped her arms around his waist. "Do you mean it?"

"I do. It's not at all what I envisioned, but I love it. It's perfect. It's us. Don't you think?"

"Yes, I do think so. And your tongue-in-cheek marketing."

Someone behind them called out, "Speech. Speech."

He chuckled and turned to face his guests. "Thank you all for coming. All I'll say is that if you see something awesome coming from this garage, it's a miracle."

His guests laughed and clapped. Happiness rolled over him in waves.

Then, the sound of motorcycles filled the air and his stomach twisted. Ten bikes rolled to a stop on the street and the bikers slowly sauntered toward the garage. He whispered to Grace. "Get your phone ready, just in case."

"Okay."

He moved through the crowd toward the bikers, hoping to stop them before they entered his property.

The leader of the group looked into his eyes and grinned.

"Looks like it's official."

Sid only nodded.

"We're here to celebrate this new endeavor in your life."

Sid shook his head. "Nope. You're not allowed."

"Why not. Your sign over there..." He pointed to a handmade sign out front. "Public welcome."

"Except for you. Your shenanigans here in town make you not welcome."

He barked out a laugh. "Shenanigans?"

"You know what I mean."

"No, I don't." He turned and nodded to his biker friends and they all walked onto the property and began tipping tables over. People scrambled and food was tossed on the ground. One of the bikers pulled out a gun and fired it in the air. The townspeople screamed and scrambled for cover. Not Sid. He was truly enraged and sick of these assholes creating this fear and havoc. He stepped closer to the leader of the gang and looked him in the eye. "Get the fuck off my property."

The man simply laughed at him. "I'm not going anywhere. I heard your woman over there got the city council to make things tough for us. But, guess what, we ain't going anywhere."

Sirens sounded and Sid's lips spread into a smile. "We'll see."

Two squad cars pulled to a stop and the two officers got out of their squads and began arresting the bikers. Quinn and Jace helped officers handcuff the bikers, each forcing the bikers to the ground on their knees until officers could read them their rights and get them transported. More sirens sounded as police from the neighboring town of Brookstown pulled to a stop.

Sid turned to find Grace, but what caught his attention was one of Quinn's guys sitting on the ground, shaking, the blank stare in his eyes. He was having a PTSD attack. Sid called Chiefy over to him. He petted her coat and whispered to her to calm her down. "I need your help, girl." He crooned.

Sid and Chiefy slowly approached the man on the ground. Sid sat next to him and Chiefy did what she did. She laid across his legs, hoping her weight would make him better.

After a few moments, Sid spoke evenly and softly to the young man. "Chiefy here has helped me through a few episodes like you're having now. She's very good at it. And, frankly a source of pride to her."

The man swallowed and sniffed. "I'm weak."

"No, you aren't. You've been through trauma and have seen things many don't have to see. You've served your country honorably and sadly, that takes a toll many will never understand. But I do. And Chiefy here does too."

Slowly the man lifted his hand and started slowly petting Chiefy. Sid sat quietly, making sure Chiefy was safe and the man was beginning to come through his PTSD attack.

Sid swallowed and glanced up to see Grace standing a

few yards away watching them. She nodded and smiled at him and he nodded in return. The chaos around them had begun to subside. The police were hauling the bikers away and the area was cleared to ensure no one was injured. A couple people had tripped running away, one woman had a scraped elbow. But generally, other than being scared, folks were fine.

As the young man shook off his attack, Sid held his hand out to him. "Sid Hoffman."

The man smiled and shook his hand. "Hayes Brooks."

Sid made sure Hayes was good before he released Chiefy from her work. He petted her and gave her a couple of snacks. "You're the best girl, Chiefy. I sure do love you," he praised.

Grace neared and chuckled. "I'm getting jealous."

Sid laughed. "I can't help it, she's just that good."

Grace stared into his eyes. "That was a great thing you just did, Sid."

He swallowed. "Thanks. He needed my help. And Chiefy's."

She smiled sweetly. "And did you also notice you didn't need Chiefy's help?"

He stared into her blue eyes. They were clear and beautiful, his new favorite color. "I guess I didn't notice it at the time but now that you mention it, I do."

"I'm proud of you, Sid."

He fished in his pocket for the most precious chunk of gold and diamond he'd ever carried. He got down on one knee and held it out to Grace. "Grace. Will you do me the honor of marrying me?"

He saw a tear slide down her cheek. Her tongue swept out and licked her lips and she swallowed. "Yes. I'd be honored to be your wife."

The few remaining people clapped their hands as he slipped the ring on her finger, then stood to kiss her lips and make it official.

His friends, Quinn and Jace congratulated them. Chiefy jumped around like she understood what was happening.

He looked at Grace. "I'm only going to hire veterans here at the Garage when I need to. I can help others too. It's something I never dreamed I'd be able to do, but you've loved me so much, you've healed me."

She chuckled and took a deep breath. "I do love you. But, honey, it was you who healed yourself. I've only been honored to witness it."

"We're going to need to set a wedding date. I say next month."

She laughed. "I can't think of a better month to marry."

He turned his head to Quinn and Jace. "You guys hear that. We're getting married next month."

Quinn laughed. "We heard. We'll spread the word you're off the market."

Jace chuckled. "Let me offer you this engagement gift. Officer Moody told me they weren't letting the bikers out of jail until they each paid a five thousand dollar fine. Since a firearm was discharged, it escalated the fines. Afterwards, the police are going to highly recommend they leave town."

Sid squeezed Grace. "That's a great engagement gift."

Quinn slapped Sid on the back and leaned over and hugged Grace. "Thank you for loving my friend."

Grace smiled. "I thank you for all the years you've had his six."

Quinn grinned. "Always."

Sid glanced over and saw Coop sitting at a table. He tugged Grace's hand and pulled her over to him.

"Are you alright, Coop?" He asked.

His old wrinkled eyes looked between him and Grace. "Yep. I'm proud of you Sid. You stood up to those bikers and you're finally making this woman your wife."

"Yep. That's the best part of today."

Coop nodded. His old blue eyes looked at Grace, a crooked grin lifted one side of his lips. Coop nodded at Grace. "You're a great partner for Sid. You two will do well together."

Grace smiled at Coop. "Thank you. I think he's a great partner for me."

Coop shrugged. "It doesn't make a difference. What matters is you always work together like you've done with these bastards here today."

Grace looked into his eyes. "I will. I promise."

Sid kissed her forehead. "I promise as well."

Grace wrapped her arm around his waist. "Why don't we get married here in the parking lot of Miracle Garage?"

"What?" He pulled his head back and looked into her eyes. "Why?"

Grace chuckled. "It's where we met. You were sitting right there." She pointed to the Knucklehead.

"But, I wasn't exactly at my best."

"You were real."

He swallowed the hot lump that formed in his throat and took a deep breath. He didn't think he could say anything so he stared into her eyes and nodded.

Are you excited to find out who heals Quinn's broken heart? get your copy of Sultry Nights here.

Sultry Nights - https://www.pjfiala.com/product/sultry-nights-eb/

Let's keep in touch and learn about new releases, sales, and other fun things by signing up for my newsletter - https://www.subscribepage.com/PJsReadersClub_copy

ALSO BY PJ FIALA

I'm fortunate to be able to do what I love. It's a blessing.

My list of written works has gotten so long I needed to move it to my website! How's that for blessed?

Anyway, click the link below to see the list of all of my books.

Thank you so much for reading.

Click here to see a list of all of my books with the blurbs.

If you're reading a paperback, go to -

https://www.pjfiala.com/bibliography-pj-fiala/

MEET PJ

Writing has been a desire my whole life. Once I found the courage to write, life changed for me in the most profound way. Bringing stories to readers that I'd enjoy reading and creating characters that are flawed, but lovable is such a joy.

When not writing, I'm with my family doing something fun. My husband, Gene, and I are bikers and enjoy riding to new locations, meeting new people and generally enjoying this fabulous country we live in.

I come from a family of veterans. My grandfather, father, brother, two sons, and one daughter-in-law are all veterans. Needless to say, I am proud to be an American and proud of the service my amazing family has given.

My online home is https://www.pjfiala.com.
You can connect with me on
Facebook: https://www.facebook.com/PJFialaAuthor
Instagram: https://www.Instagram.com/PJFiala.
YouTube: https://youtube.com/@PJFiala
TikTok: https://www.tiktok.com/@pjfiala?lang=en
If you prefer to email, go ahead, I'll respond - pjfiala@ pjfiala.com.

COPYRIGHT

Printed in the United States of America
First published 2024
Fiala, PJ
Steamy Nights / PJ Fiala
p. cm.
1. Romance—Fiction. 2. Romance—Suspense. 3. Romance - Military
I. Title – Steamy Nights

www.ingramcontent.com/pod-product-compliance
Lightning Source LLC
Chambersburg PA
CBHW070416310726
48977CB00003B/711